MY ENEMY, MY ROMEO

A FORBIDDEN CRIME FAMILY ROMANCE

My Enemy, My Romeo
A Forbidden Crime Family Romance

Magness Studies
Second Edition, 2026
Originally Published as Starcross: A Modern Romeo and Juliet Romance
Printed in the United States of America
ISBN: 979-8-9934400-9-5

Prologue. Federal Interview Room — Washington, D.C.

"State your name for the record."

Benvolio looked down at his hands and saw blood dried into the lines of his skin. Some of it was his. Some of it belonged to his friend.

The interview room was built to make men small and help break them down: gray walls, gray table, gray metal door. A recorder sat between him and the two agents across from him, its red light steady and obscene. Benvolio had not asked to wash up. No one had offered.

He lifted the paper cup slightly, heard it tap softly against the table, and set it back down before the shaking showed too clearly.

"My name is Benvolio Omerti," he said. His voice sounded scraped raw. "Special Agent, Federal Bureau of Investigation."

"Omerti," the man across from him said. "But your mother was a Montague."

Benvolio's jaw tightened. "Yes."

"Salvatore Montague's family."

"Yes."

"The Italian Mafia family operating through East Coast ports, labor contracts, private security, and political money in Washington."

"That's one way to say it."

"What's another?"

Benvolio fixed his gaze on the recorder. "Family."

The woman across from him paused, her pen hovering over the page.

The man folded his hands. "So explain how a man with Montague blood becomes an FBI agent."

Benvolio gave an exhale that almost became a laugh. "With difficulty."

No one smiled.

"Nothing else? Nothing else you would like to discuss besides 'it was difficult'?"

"No," Benvolio said. "Nothing else is relevant."

The man leaned back. "Careful, Agent Omerti."

Benvolio stared at the blood on his hands again. "I have been careful all my life while others have been reckless. Maybe that is why I am still alive, or maybe I have just been lucky."

Quiet gathered under the steady red light of the recorder.

"You walked in both worlds," the woman said.

Benvolio nodded once. "Neither side liked it."

"But both used it."

"Yes."

"The Bureau used your family access."

"Yes."

"And the Montagues?"

"They used the fact that I was still family when it suited them."

"And when it didn't?"

"Then I was a fed."

The man waited a moment. "And your motive for being an FBI agent?"

Benvolio looked up.

"It's complicated and personal," he said. "But it doesn't really apply to what happened today, does it?"

"That depends on how honest you intend to be."

Benvolio lowered his eyes to his hands. "I wanted peace," he said at last. "Or something close enough that people might stop dying long enough to mistake it for peace."

"By serving both sides?"

"By standing between them." His voice roughened. "There is a difference."

"Is there?"

"There was supposed to be."

The man across from him regarded him. "And the Kapulets?"

Benvolio's eyes lifted. "Viktor Kapulet. Russian money. Freight routes. Private security. Diplomatic friends. Properties held through shell companies clean enough to pass a bank review and dirty enough to keep this office awake."

Neither agent answered.

"Russian Mafia," Benvolio said.

No one spoke for a beat. Then the woman asked whether Benvolio understood why he was there tonight. Benvolio let out a short laugh that did not sound like him. He understood why he was in the building. He understood the blood on his shirt. He understood that his friend was dead—one of many, by the time the city finished counting its losses and choosing which ones mattered. What he did not understand was how any of them had thought this would stay manageable.

The woman's voice softened by one careful degree. "Start where you can."

Benvolio looked past her at the black observation glass. Internal review. Supervisors. Lawyers. Everyone waiting for a clean sequence and a cleaner explanation than the city had earned. He had one that none of them would like. Benvolio rubbed his thumb over the side of one finger and watched the tremor return.

"It started a year ago," he said. "With Rosaline. And a letter."

The woman looked up. "A letter?"

Benvolio saw the envelope in his mind before he answered. Cream paper. An old-fashioned wax seal.

"Who was the letter for?"

Benvolio fixed his gaze on the recorder and answered without blinking.

"Juliet Kapulet."

Chapter 1. One Year Earlier, Late Night — Northwest Washington, D.C.

Rosaline's mouth opened under his in the warm gold dimness of her apartment. Romeo had one hand braced beside her head and the other spread at her waist, feeling the heat of her through the thin cotton twisted halfway up her body, feeling the way she arched into him like she had already stopped pretending she meant to keep this playful. Rain ticked faintly at the window. The bedside lamp burned low. Her room smelled of skin, perfume, and the designer candle she never let burn all the way down because, according to Rosaline, endings should be chosen, not wasted.

He kissed her again, slower this time, and she answered with a low sound that emptied his head of every decent thought he had left. She was beautiful in the way some women made beauty feel like a weapon they had never bothered to sheath. Olive skin warm with want. Black hair spilled in dark waves across the pillow. Dark eyes half-lidded until he looked too directly and saw amusement sharpen there. Rosaline always knew exactly what effect she was having and would have been offended by any man too stupid to notice.

"You're staring," she murmured.

"You're talking," he said against her throat. "That feels ungrateful."

She laughed softly and hooked one leg higher around his hip. "You say that like I owe you silence."

"Not silence." He kissed the line of her jaw, then lower, where her pulse jumped under his mouth. "Something more primal."

"That sounds like a personal fantasy."

He smiled despite himself. That was Rosaline. She never surrendered the cutting edges entirely—not even like this, not even half beneath him with one hand in his hair and her breathing already quickening. She made pleasure feel like a conversation she intended to win. Romeo slid his hand higher beneath the rumpled hem of her camisole. She shivered.

The wit in her face shifted first. Her eyes closed for one second. When they opened again, the amusement in them had gone darker, replaced by hunger.

"There," she said, her voice lower now. "Better."

He kissed her properly then. Not the teasing version. Not the half-laughing, half-fighting one they had been circling through for the last ten minutes. Rosaline's fingers tightened in his hair. His weight settled more firmly between her thighs. The mattress shifted beneath them with the slow, intimate friction of bodies.

Her skin was hot under his palm. Her mouth hotter. When he moved against her, just enough to feel her answer him, she exhaled, the sound trembling at the end, and said, “Romeo.”

Hearing his name like that nearly finished him by itself. He drew back only enough to look at her. His own breathing had gone uneven. His shirt was half open, tie long gone, cuffs unbuttoned. Rosaline was flushed from throat to chest, one strap slipped down her shoulder, the edge of black lace visible where her camisole had twisted. She looked wrecked already and nowhere near enough.

“If you keep looking at me like that,” she said, “I’m going to assume you’ve lost whatever manners your family gave you.”

“Rosaline,” he said quietly, “my family has nothing to do with the thoughts I’m having right now.”

That brought the slow, wicked smile he had been hoping for.

“No?” she asked, with a quirk of her red lips.

“No.”

“Good.” She smiled, biting her lower lip. She lifted her head, opened her mouth, and kissed him.

Romeo swore under his breath and kissed her harder. One hand slid up her thigh. The other moved to the small of her back and pulled her fully against him. She rose to meet him with a startled inhale, and for a few perfect seconds there was nothing left in the room but heat, pressure, and the deepening certainty that neither of them was going to stop. They hungered for each other. Then the alarm went off, splitting the room apart.

Rosaline froze beneath him. Romeo shut his eyes and dropped his forehead to her shoulder while the phone on the nightstand began shrieking into the dark room.

“No,” Rosaline said, as if her words would pause time and return her to where she and Romeo had been.

Romeo laughed once, helpless and wrecked. “Ignore it.”

“No,” she said again, reaching blindly toward the nightstand while the alarm kept blaring. “No, I have a job. I need to be responsible.”

“I would prefer you not to be.”

She found the phone, silenced it, and let her arm fall back to the mattress with dramatic despair. For a heartbeat, neither of them moved, and the quiet after the alarm was worse. It left all the unfinished wanting in place and sharpened it with interruption. Romeo was still half over her, still aroused, still trying to steady himself. Rosaline looked up at him with equal frustration written plainly across her face.

"This," she said, "is hateful."

"It is."

"We could ignore it," he said.

"We could," she replied. "And then in an hour I'd still have to go, only hedonistically satisfied, but with more real-world problems."

"I'm leaning more toward hedonistically satisfied," he replied with a devilish grin.

Rosaline rolled her eyes, amusement tugging at the corners of her mouth despite herself. "You don't have people relying on you."

Romeo rolled onto his back with a muttered curse and dragged a hand over his face. Rosaline sat up beside him and pushed her hair back off her shoulders. For a foolish second, he forgot annoyance entirely and just watched her. She caught him at it.

"That expression," she said, "is not helping me become responsible."

"Like I said, I prefer you not to be."

"That," Rosaline said, swinging her legs over the side of the bed, "is one of your ruder qualities."

They dressed in the awkward, dissatisfied rush of people dragged away from exactly what they still wanted most. Romeo shoved his shirt back on without caring whether the buttons lined up properly. Rosaline stepped into her jeans and reached for her blouse, her skin still flushed and her black hair still unruly. One look at her was enough to make him think very obscene, very impractical things about how quickly they could abandon the whole effort and fall back into bed. She saw the thought on his face and pointed at him.

"No."

"That's cruel."

"Get over it."

He caught her wrist as she passed and pulled her close enough to steal one rough kiss that made both of them regret behaving at all. By the time they made it out of the apartment and halfway down the stairs, Rosaline stopped so abruptly Romeo nearly walked into her.

"What?"

"The letter."

He stared at her. "The whole point of us leaving now is letters. You're a courier."

"Not for long," Rosaline replied. "I gave my two weeks' notice. Let's just say I had a disagreement with my boss."

Romeo frowned. "Wait a minute. Paris Sokol? That boss? The most eligible bachelor in D.C.?" He paused, the thought catching up with him. "And you quit?"

Then his expression shifted, hopeful and wicked.

"In that case, let's just get back in bed."

Rosaline shook her head. "Yeah, I don't want to talk about it. But I need to get the other letter. That's the important one. The one I need to be responsible for."

"You are speaking in riddles, and I am already frustrated."

Rosaline was turning back toward the apartment. "Don't sound like that. It's unattractive."

He followed her upstairs again as she crossed straight to the desk by the window. From beneath a book, she lifted a cream envelope sealed with old-fashioned wax and slipped it into her bag with a care that immediately sharpened his attention.

"That one matters," he said.

"Yes."

"For work?"

Rosaline hesitated, and the pause told him more than the answer would have.

"No," she said. "That one's for Juliet."

Romeo shut the apartment door behind them and followed her back down the stairs. "Juliet who?"

Rosaline glanced over her shoulder. "You really have never met her."

"That sounds suspicious. Why wouldn't I have met her?"

"It's complicated," she said. "Also history. We were friends before we drifted apart. Your families are also ridiculous."

They reached the car and got in, bringing the last of the apartment's warmth and frustration with them. Romeo started the engine. Rosaline set her bag by her feet and rested one hand lightly over it where the letter sat inside.

"Explain," he said.

"Juliet Kapulet."

Romeo glanced at her, then back to the windshield. "Kapulet."

"Yes."

"That seems like the kind of detail one leads with, especially when you are sharing a bed with a Montague."

"You never asked."

"My family and hers barely say each other's names in daylight."

Rosaline leaned her head back against the seat. "Exactly. Which is one reason you've never met her. The second is that we haven't been friends for a while."

He pulled out into the wet Washington street. Streetlights smeared gold over the windshield. "You were friends with a Kapulet?"

"I was friends with Juliet."

"They are basically the same thing."

"Not exactly," Rosaline said. "Juliet is a Kapulet, but she doesn't buy into the whole family thing. She's—or at least she was—my best friend. She's smart, funny, and loyal."

Romeo glanced at her. "If she is so loyal, then why aren't you friends anymore? And why are you writing and then carrying a note to her?"

"As for the notes, that had always been our thing. We used to joke that the calligraphy and wax seals made them fancy and glamorous, and probably the most secure method of communication," she said. "I thought it would be a nice gesture as I try to mend that bridge."

"What happened?" Romeo asked.

She looked out the side window briefly before continuing. "That is between her and me."

"You're being mysterious, and with a Kapulet, no less."

"Your families feud constantly," she said. "And every man involved insists it's about business, history, leverage, pride, contracts, respect, territory, or some other grave masculine word meant to make stupidity sound important."

Romeo drove one block without answering. Then he said, "It's business."

Rosaline turned toward him fully. "There. Do you hear yourself?"

"You're right," he said. "Shipping, labor, money, politics, old loyalties, criminal ego dressed up as civic necessity. That doesn't make it noble. It just makes it real."

"And petty," she said.

"And volatile."

"That too."

For a short while, the city moved around them in wet light and shadow. Then Rosaline shifted closer across the console. Romeo felt her before he turned toward her. The frustration from the bed had not gone anywhere. It had only changed shape. He could still remember the heat of her under him, the sound she had made when he touched her, the fact that both of them had been so close to satisfaction, only to be denied by the crushing weight of responsibility. It was frustrating, to say the least. Rosaline leaned in and kissed the edge of his ear.

Romeo's grip on the wheel tightened instantly. "Rosaline."

"What?" she asked mischievously.

Then her mouth moved to his neck.

He inhaled once. "I'm driving."

"Yes."

"That was not an invitation."

"It was not a refusal either."

She kissed him again, slower this time, and let her teeth catch just enough to make his whole body go taut, heat rushing low through him.

"This is cruel," he muttered.

"Yes," she said. "But gracefully so." The edges of her mouth curled, and the hunger in her eyes deepened.

Her hand settled lightly at his chest, then lower—not claiming, just reminding him of exactly what had been interrupted and how easily she could keep him there for the rest of the drive. He laughed once under his breath, half wrecked already.

"You're incorrigible."

"And yet," Rosaline murmured.

A horn tore across the intersection, and Romeo's head snapped toward the sound. A delivery truck was already in the intersection, running the light, its headlights flooding the windshield in one violent burst of white. He jerked the wheel on instinct. Rosaline had time for one startled inhale, one snapped cry—and then the truck hit.

Metal folded inward. Glass burst across the cab. The steering column wrenched under his hands. Rosaline's body slammed sideways into the passenger door. The world became impact, noise, and the violent collapse of motion into ruin. Then the horn kept screaming from somewhere inside the wreck. Romeo tasted copper.

For a stunned instant, he could not understand. Lights and sounds blurred together, and thought would not settle. The windshield was a white cracked web. Cold air poured through the shattered passenger side. His ears rang so fiercely the whole world sounded far away. Then he turned.

"Rosaline."

The passenger side had taken the full force of the strike. Her head was angled against the broken frame of the window, black hair tangled with safety glass, olive skin draining fast beneath the blood at her temple and neck. Her bag had split open at her feet. The cream envelope lay half exposed, the address still visible.

"Rosaline."

This time his voice came out shredded. He reached for her with both shaking hands as strangers started running toward the car through the Washington dark.

Chapter 2. Tuesday Morning — Outside the Federal Courthouse, Washington, D.C.

The morning outside the federal courthouse had the brittle, cutting cold Washington did so well in late fall. The sky was pale and unforgiving. Wind cut through wool. Damp from the night before still slicked the sidewalks. Reporters clustered behind metal barricades with coffee in gloved hands while camera crews shifted for angles and courthouse deputies watched the crowd with the dull suspicion of men who expected trouble and hated being right. Benvolio saw it beginning before anyone else admitted it was happening.

He was halfway across the street when he noticed two Kapulet security men near the curb. They stood a little too loose, spoke a little too loudly, and laughed just far enough beyond professionalism to make the sound carry. Both wore dark tailored coats and the blank expressions of men who wanted very badly to be underestimated. Ten yards away, two contractors tied to a Montague security outfit waited beside a black SUV, watching them with the stubborn poise that usually came right before something stupid. Benvolio adjusted his pace and kept watching.

It wasn't the setup that bothered him. D.C. was built on staged proximity—rivals pushed through the same hallways, the same fundraisers, the same courthouse steps. It was the energy between them. Too direct. Too interested. Like the men had shown up hoping for an excuse. One of the Kapulet guards said something in Russian. The second laughed.

One of the Montague contractors, a younger man Benvolio only knew as Larson, turned his head. "You got something to say, say it in English."

The first Kapulet guard met his eyes and smiled. It was the kind of smile that tightened Benvolio's jaw immediately—unfriendly, unhurried, calculated enough to insult. The guard repeated himself in English, slower this time. Something about Italian suits and union boys both being cheap if you knew the right docks to buy them at. Ricci, the older contractor beside Larson, muttered for him to leave it alone. Larson didn't.

He stepped forward. "Say it again."

The Kapulet guard spread his hands in a mockery of innocence. "You think everything is about you?"

Then he bumped Larson's shoulder as he passed. It took little effort, and under better circumstances, it should have ended there. It didn't. Larson shoved him. The Kapulet guard shoved back. The second Russian stepped in a second later, and Ricci moved because once fists started flying there was no leaving another man alone in front of cameras and courthouse deputies. Benvolio cursed under his breath and broke into a run.

By the time he hit the curb, one of the Kapulet men had Larson by the coat and was driving him backward into the barricade. Ricci was grappling with the other, both of them slipping on wet pavement while reporters shouted for their cameramen and deputies started forward too cautiously to matter. A woman in heels stumbled trying to get clear.

"Break it up!" Benvolio barked.

He grabbed Ricci first and yanked him off balance with enough force to tear him free. Ricci recognized him and let go at once. That should have ended the fight; at least, that was what Benvolio hoped. Instead, it opened it wider.

The second Kapulet guard swung toward Benvolio. Benvolio knocked the arm aside and shoved him backward into the SUV with enough force to rattle the door. Larson took that as his chance and lunged again. Someone shouted. Someone else slammed hard enough into the hood to leave a dent. Then Tybalt Kapulet arrived.

He came down the courthouse annex steps like violence had summoned him personally. His dark coat was open, gloves in one hand, expression already sharpened with contempt. He was younger than the men around him, but command sat on him more naturally than restraint ever would have. He took in the deputies, the cameras, the contractors, and Benvolio in the middle of the mess with one sweep of his gaze. His mouth curved, not into a smile, but into something worse.

"What is this?" he asked.

It was not a real question. It was an accusation dressed as curiosity.

Benvolio stepped in front of him before he could move deeper into the fight. "Stand down."

Tybalt's gaze dropped briefly to Benvolio's FBI credentials, then lifted again. "You telling me what to do on a public sidewalk now?"

"I'm telling you this ends here."

Tybalt laughed softly. It was the delighted sound of a man who had just found the exact kind of resistance he enjoyed most. "That's the problem with your people," he said. "You think a badge makes you real."

Tybalt gestured toward the courthouse deputies. "Do you think they care what happens to you?"

Behind Benvolio, another shove turned into a crash against the barricades. One of the reporters shouted something about getting the shot. A deputy finally reached for his radio.

Tybalt looked past Benvolio toward his own men, then back again. "If you want it to stop, stop them."

He moved then. Not toward Benvolio, but sideways—toward Ricci, where the oldest bruise in the room looked easiest to deepen. A small silver flash appeared in his hand so quickly it barely registered before Benvolio understood what he was seeing. A knife. Benvolio caught Tybalt's wrist before the blade landed.

The impact drove both of them into the SUV with enough force to shake the windows. Tybalt twisted instantly, all trained reflex and ugly purpose, turning the knife for leverage instead of show. Up close he smelled faintly of coffee and expensive cologne, his face composed with the cold excitement of a man who genuinely enjoyed the instant when order gave way to violence.

"Put it down," Benvolio said through his teeth.

"Make me."

Benvolio slammed his forearm into Tybalt's shoulder and knocked his wrist against the doorframe. The knife hit the pavement and skidded under the bumper. Tybalt struck back immediately—disciplined and vicious.

The deputies closed in at last, shouting for everyone to get down, but the crowd had already shifted into the ugly shape public violence always made—half retreat, half fascination. Then the sirens got louder.

A government sedan slid to the curb, followed by another, and the atmosphere changed before the doors even opened. U.S. Attorney Escalus stepped out with two federal marshals behind him, and nothing about him suggested drama. That was part of what made him effective. Tybalt liked spectacle. Escalus didn't need it. He carried authority the way other people carried umbrellas—out of habit and with no intention of putting it down.

"What the hell is this?" he snapped.

The question cut across the sidewalk louder than the wind. Everyone froze. Tybalt stilled in Benvolio's grip. The contractors backed off just enough to look less guilty than they had a second earlier. Deputies straightened. Reporters leaned forward like sharks scenting prey.

Escalus took in the fight, the cameras, the knife on the ground, the men breathing heavily in tailored coats. His gaze stopped on Benvolio.

"Agent Omerti."

Benvolio released Tybalt and stepped back. "Public disturbance escalating toward aggravated violence," he responded. "We were containing it."

Tybalt gave a short laugh at that. Escalus turned on him so fast the sound died unfinished.

"You find this funny?"

Tybalt said nothing.

Escalus looked from one side to the other, fury settling colder instead of louder. "Let me make this very clear. I do not care whose last name bought influence in this city, or whose lawyers think they can call my office directly. You turn a federal courthouse into a street brawl again, I will charge every breathing idiot involved so aggressively your grandchildren will still be appealing it."

Nobody answered. One camera crew edged closer. A marshal shut that down with one cold look.

Escalus kept going. "This city is not your private battleground. Not yours. Not yours. Not yours." He pointed as he said it—to the contractors, to the Kapulet detail, to Tybalt, and finally to Benvolio too, which Benvolio did not appreciate but understood. "If I see violence over pride one more time, I will make an example out of all of you."

Pride hadn't vanished. Tybalt was still Tybalt. But public threats created paper trails, and paper trails were harder to kill than witnesses. The contractors stepped back. The deputies moved in. The pressure on the sidewalk dropped from active violence to deferred threat.

Tybalt bent slowly and retrieved his gloves. He did not look at the knife. One of the marshals had already kicked it farther away. When Tybalt lifted his eyes to Benvolio again, the heat in them was gone. Rage would have been easier to read. What Benvolio saw instead was patience. A promise saved for later. Then Tybalt turned and walked away. The fight was over, but the conflict was not.

As the crowd loosened and the cameras chased fresh angles, Salvatore Montague came down the courthouse steps with the quiet gravity of a man who had spent his life being obeyed without ever needing to raise his voice. Everything about him was measured—his coat, his expression, the measured pace of his steps. He looked over the scene with visible disgust, then shifted his attention to Benvolio.

Ellis, Salvatore's weathered retainer and driver, kept half a step behind him with the patience of a man who had spent years holding doors for bad news and pretending not to hear what passed through them.

"Have you seen my son this morning?" Salvatore asked.

Benvolio shook his head. "No, sir."

Salvatore gave one short nod, but his jaw tightened. He was not a man prone to open concern, which made the strain around his eyes show more sharply.

Salvatore tolerated Benvolio in the peculiar Washington way powerful men reserved for family problems they could not cleanly discard. Benvolio was Romeo's cousin, which made him difficult to remove entirely, but he was still Agent Omerti to the Bureau and the Montagues alike—too federal to embrace, too Montague to ignore.

"If you do," Salvatore said, "tell him I was looking for him."

Then he turned and went back inside before Benvolio could answer.

Romeo Montague had been drifting since Rosaline died. On paper he was still functional, still holding his place inside the family machine. But Benvolio knew him too well and so did his father. There was distance in him now, something inward and half broken, as if he had survived the visible wreck and died in the invisible one. Benvolio found him near the canal in Georgetown a little before ten.

Romeo stood by the railing with one hand in his pocket and the other braced on cold iron, staring down at the water like it had personally disappointed him. Washington moved around him in layers—traffic in the distance, joggers passing, a dog barking somewhere across the path—but none of it seemed to touch him.

When Benvolio called to him, Romeo glanced back over his shoulder and offered a smile so practiced it made Benvolio want to hit something.

"You miss the show?" Romeo asked.

"You mean the courthouse fight?"

"I mean Washington embarrassing itself before lunch."

Benvolio came to stand beside him. "Your father was looking for you."

"Was he?"

"Yes."

Romeo turned to the water. "And?"

"And what?"

"And did he sound disappointed, angry, concerned, or just professionally inconvenienced?"

Benvolio gave him a sidelong look. "It was not your fault. You shouldn't keep torturing yourself."

That got a real reaction. Romeo laughed once, but there was no humor in it. "That obvious?"

"To me."

Romeo rubbed a hand over his jaw and returned his gaze to the water. The wind lifted a lock of dark hair off his forehead and moved the collar of his coat. He did not look tired in any simple physical way; it went deeper than that. Something inside him had worn thin and not healed.

"It's not just my father," he said at last. "It's everything after Rosaline."

Benvolio stayed silent. He had read the police reports. It was a hit-and-run accident, but it was odd. The truck was found several blocks down the road, abandoned. No one had been held accountable for Rosaline's death, but it was apparent to everyone who loved him, even his parents, that he relived it every day.

Romeo kept his eyes on the black water below. "Everybody wants me back in motion. Back in the role of the heir of a family. Back in the suit. Like mourning is a scheduling problem." He exhaled through his nose. "And I keep carrying something I should have put into the right hands months ago."

Benvolio's gaze dropped briefly to the inside pocket of Romeo's coat. "The letter."

"Yes."

"You still haven't found a way?"

Romeo shook his head. "A Montague doesn't send a note to a Kapulet daughter and expect it to arrive unopened. Tybalt would burn it. Her parents would bury it. Mailing it would be worse."

He rubbed his thumb once over the seam of the pocket. "I'm tired of being whatever everyone else needs. Son. Heir. Asset. Reassurance." His expression tightened. "I'm tired all the way through, Ben."

Benvolio watched him. It wasn't only family pressure. It was grief stripped of ceremony and forced back into tailored clothes. It was a man trying to carry the dead honestly inside a world that kept asking for a performance of the living version instead. And it was exactly the kind of exhaustion that made one bad decision look like hope in disguise.

Chapter 3. Tuesday Afternoon — Georgetown, Washington, D.C.

By midafternoon, Georgetown had gone gray and cut thin by winter, every window catching the light just long enough to look rich before dark took it back. Benvolio and Romeo walked from a coffee shop down one of the quieter residential streets, a paper cup cooling in Benvolio's hand. Benvolio had stopped drinking from it ten minutes earlier. The caffeine, the remains of the courthouse mess, and Romeo's steady melancholy had left him feeling restless in body and spirit alike. A side gate of the neighboring property opened.

A courier stepped out with a cream envelope in one hand and a typed admissions sheet clipped beneath it. He looked young, harried, and already overmatched by the block he was standing on. He checked the brass numbers on the townhouse, looked back at the envelope, then at the list, and muttered something under his breath about rich people, paper invitations, and addresses apparently arranged by the devil himself. Romeo noticed first.

"You look lost," he said.

The courier startled and glanced between them, trying to decide whether they were making fun of him.

"I have the right neighborhood," he said. "I may not have the right house."

Romeo stepped closer and glanced toward the numbers on the row of townhouses. "Who are you looking for?"

The man looked down at the page. "Vale. Mercutio Vale."

Benvolio straightened slightly.

Romeo held out a hand. "Let me see."

The staffer hesitated, then passed him the list and the envelope together, too stressed to be cautious. Romeo scanned the typed page first. Final admissions. Seating notes. Guest confirmations. At the top, in formal print: KAPULET WINTER MASQUERADE IN HONOR OF JULIET KAPULET. Romeo's eyes moved lower. Half the city was on the list. Senators. Donors. Embassy wives. Committee chairs. And there, several entries down, sat Mercutio Vale. He stilled.

The staffer mistook it for concentration. "You know the house?"

"Yes," Romeo said.

He handed the sheet back and pointed down the block. "Second corner, then left at the iron gate with the stone lions. Vale's not in this row. He's in the hotel residence annex off the next street."

The courier looked relieved enough to kiss him. "Thank you."

Benvolio, now paying much closer attention, said, "Big night?"

The man gave a tired laugh. "Kapulet masquerade. Their daughter. Everybody with money or influence wants to be seen having been invited. Nobody wants to help the poor bastard carrying the paper."

Then he hurried off in the direction Romeo had indicated. Benvolio waited until the man had turned the corner. Then he turned to Romeo.

"No."

Romeo kept his eyes on the now-empty stretch of sidewalk. "I didn't say anything."

"You didn't have to."

Romeo turned at last. "Mercutio's invited."

"Yes," Benvolio said. "I can read chaos from a distance too."

Romeo exhaled through his nose. "It's a masquerade for Juliet."

Benvolio stared at him. "And?"

"And Tybalt would never let a Montague near her in daylight."

"That sounds like the beginning of wisdom."

"But Mercutio can walk into almost any room in Washington."

Benvolio shut his eyes briefly. "There it is."

Romeo stayed silent, which was worse.

Benvolio lowered his voice. "No. I know that look. This is a horrible idea. Just have Mercutio give her the letter. You already said they won't stop him."

Romeo turned fully toward him now.

"No," he said. "This is something I have to do. No—it's something I need to do. I need to give Juliet the letter. It was the last thing Rosaline wanted. I owe that to her."

The anguish sat too close to the surface, too easy to read on a face trained from birth to hide pain behind breeding and composure. Benvolio weighed the words. Then, with a pit of dread opening in his stomach, he gave the smallest nod. They were really going to do this.

They found Mercutio three blocks over in the back booth of a hotel bar, already dressed for the evening and arguing with the bartender about martinis before five.

Mercutio Vale had been born for official photographs. He was Escalus's younger cousin, handsome in the polished, infuriating way that made older women call him promising and younger women lust after him. The family had expected him to play the good son—law school, donor dinners, and eventually some respectable public life designed to look like service and feel like inheritance. Mercutio had joined the Army to spite them instead.

He came home with a bad-conduct discharge, a sharper mouth, and the permanent conviction that any role handed to him by better people deserved to be worn incorrectly.

He listened to Romeo's story without interrupting: the lost courier, the admissions list, the masquerade in Juliet's honor, Mercutio listed on the page, Rosaline's letter still in Romeo's pocket.

When Romeo finished, Mercutio took a slow sip of his drink and said, "So let me be sure I understand. A courier gets lost, you help him because you have a soft spot for couriers, and now you've discovered that I, through no fault of my own except birth, have become your doorway into a hostile ballroom."

"Yes," Romeo said.

Mercutio considered that. "Good. I was worried the week might remain dull."

Benvolio closed his eyes. "I had hoped you would inject a molecule of reason into this."

"Then your hopes are poorly structured in reality." Mercutio set down the glass. "Also, to be fair, this is very funny."

"It is not funny."

"It is a little funny," Mercutio said.

Romeo ignored the banter. "I never appear on the list. I go as your guest. Just long enough to get the letter into Juliet's hand."

Mercutio lifted one brow. "And if Tybalt sees you?"

"Then he sees me."

Benvolio gave him a flat look. "That is not a plan."

"No, it is not, but I do like it," Mercutio said, leaning back with the smile of a man discovering civic duty in a loaded room. "Fortunately, I am on the admissions list, and my invitation gets me two guests because somebody—inaccurately, I might add—believes I somehow improve their social standing. The fools."

"Mercutio," Benvolio said.

Mercutio ignored him and turned to Romeo instead. "Do you actually intend to hand her the letter?"

"Yes."

"Good," Mercutio said. "Anything else would be a disappointment."

Benvolio stared at both of them. "And how, exactly, would reason be a disappointment?"

"Reason is for mortgages and insurance," Mercutio said. "No one reads a book or watches a movie because it is reasonable. They want to be entertained. They want to feel alive. And this, my friends, is a quest into the very heart of your sworn enemies." He lifted his glass slightly. "Enjoy this moment, because if you have enough courage—or enough insanity—to attempt it, I can assure you of one thing: I will not be bored tonight."

Chapter 4. Tuesday Late Afternoon — Kapulet Townhouse, Georgetown

By the time Viktor Kapulet took Paris Sokol onto the rear terrace of the Georgetown townhouse, the other half of the afternoon had already begun arranging itself. Viktor preferred delicate conversations in motion. He disliked offices for anything that mattered. Offices could be monitored; after all, he had placed CCTV cameras in several rooms—the ballroom, the east parlor, his office, and a few other spaces where guests tended to forget that privacy was often an illusion. Offices also held books, paper, and the useful lie that men told the truth more readily once they had sat down across from one another.

Outside, men revealed more: the way they matched his pace, the way they handled pauses, and the way they watched the street while pretending not to. Viktor preferred paths where cameras caught glimpses rather than complete conversations—the turn of a shoulder, a hand moving too quickly, the second when a polite face forgot itself. Glimpses were useful. Whole conversations were evidence. So when Paris asked for a private word, Viktor made him wait until they were walking the length of the brick terrace behind the house the Kapulets used whenever Washington business required old-money architecture and the appearance of cultivated restraint.

The townhouse stood on a quiet Georgetown block lined with bare trees and black iron fencing. From the street, it looked dignified, expensive, and discreet. From the inside, it was wired like a fortress.

Paris wore dark wool with no overcoat, gloves tucked neatly into one pocket. He was handsome in the polished, moneyed way that looked at home on magazine covers. Good posture. Good schools. Good breeding. The sort of man families like Viktor's preferred to call safe when what they really meant was strategically valuable.

He had done the work too. Paris knew which senators Ekaterina Kapulet indulged, which donors Viktor tolerated, which schools Juliet had once brushed against and then quietly withdrawn from. He did not enter rooms blind if he could help it. He was not emotional or romantic, at least not by any honest definition. He had a plan, and he meant to see it through. They reached the far end of the terrace, where the stone wall overlooked the narrow winter garden below. Only then did Paris speak.

"I wanted to ask again about Juliet."

Viktor kept his gaze on the garden. "You have asked before."

"And I intend to keep asking."

That, at least, amused Viktor enough to earn a glance. Paris's face remained composed, but there was more tension around his mouth than usual. So this mattered. Not enough to undo him. Enough to tighten the mask.

"She is still young," Viktor said.

Paris gave a faint smile. "She's twenty-three."

"She is still young," Viktor repeated, as if the number were beside the point. "And she is mine to worry about."

Cold wind moved across the terrace, carrying damp stone and dead ivy with it. Below them, one of the security men crossed the garden path, checked the rear gate, and disappeared again. Paris folded his hands behind his back.

"I'm not asking to corner her."

That sharpened Viktor's attention more than pleading would have.

"I'm asking you not to leave her exposed longer than she has to be," Paris said. "With me, she would be safe. She would live well. She would have security, distance from the uglier parts of this city, and the kind of protection that does not fail because one man loses his temper, like this morning at the courthouse. She may not welcome the arrangement at first. Most intelligent women wouldn't. But discomfort passes. Fear doesn't."

Viktor turned his head slightly. "That sounds very civilized."

"It usually is," Paris said. "The uglier versions begin when families wait too long and call it freedom."

Viktor almost laughed.

"She doesn't have to care yet," Paris continued. "Only not refuse me before I've had the chance."

At the end of the terrace, Viktor stopped and turned to face him fully.

"That," he said, "is a better argument." He let the pause stretch between them before continuing. "You are not a fool, so let us not waste each other's time pretending this is only about affection. She is my heir. I have holdings here, and I have holdings in Europe. Through her, one day, you might stand in proxy over everything I own." His eyes held Paris's. "So tell me—why should I give you my daughter, and with her everything that follows?"

Paris held his gaze. "My motives are not difficult to understand."

"Perhaps," Viktor said. "But say them aloud."

Paris did not look away. "To expand my base. To gain access and influence in both the European and American markets. To build legitimate fronts in overseas freight, security, and insurance that will one day replace other methods." His voice remained calm. "To put it bluntly, to make enough money and command enough influence that no government, and no serious rival, would ever consider moving against me or my family."

Viktor considered him, then gave the smallest nod. "At least that is honest."

He turned slightly toward the house. "She will be at the masquerade tonight."

Paris's expression sharpened by one degree. "And?"

"And you will be there too. You will speak to her. You will charm her if you can. You will not corner her, insult her, or behave as if she is already yours." Viktor's voice stayed mild. "If she responds well, we continue. If she does not, we wait."

Paris inclined his head. "You would give me that chance?"

"I am giving you a room full of senators, diplomats, donors, and cameras," Viktor said. "If you cannot make yourself appealing in those conditions, then perhaps you are less impressive than I was told."

Paris's smile returned, restrained now. "Then I'll see her tonight."

He turned back toward the house. As he moved, Viktor could already see the evening arranging itself behind the younger man's eyes—witnesses, sight lines, pressure applied with good manners. Paris would have called that preparation. Men with less polish might have called it pursuit.

Viktor turned toward the townhouse. Music staff would already be arriving. Florists. Security teams. Caterers pretending not to notice the men with earpieces and diplomatic plates.

"She is not yet promised," he said.

Paris stopped and glanced back.

"Do not mistake invitation for possession."

"I wouldn't."

Viktor believed that exactly as much as he believed any ambitious man truly understood temperance when beauty, innocence, and advantage stood in the same doorway.

Inside the house, Ekaterina Kapulet stood at the long dining table reviewing seating cards with the same cool precision she brought to funerals, negotiations, and unpleasant family decisions.

Her dark silk blouse was immaculate. Her hair had not shifted once all day. A house manager stood at her side with a clipboard, moving only when she spoke.

"Paris?" Ekaterina asked without looking up.

"He made a better argument than he has before," Viktor said.

"And Juliet?"

Viktor glanced toward the doorway before answering. "I do not believe she is ready, nor do I believe he is ready for her. She is unruly."

Ekaterina allowed herself the faintest smirk. "That is because you coddle her, and even now you coddle her. She needs to grow up."

Viktor crossed farther into the room, glancing once over the placement cards, the silver not yet set, the flowers still waiting in their boxes to become arrangements rather than inventory. The townhouse was tightening around the evening. Staff had already begun moving with the particular speed of people trying not to look hurried in a rich home.

"At the risk of sounding sentimental, she is my daughter, Katya," Viktor said. "I would rather she act like a daughter than a bargaining chip."

Ekaterina lifted one card, considered it, and moved it two places farther down the table. Only then did she look at him.

"She is both," she said.

Viktor offered no reply. That pause did not discourage Ekaterina. If anything, it made her surer of her footing.

"At her age, I knew exactly what my parents expected of me," she said. "I may not have liked it, but I understood it. Juliet is intelligent enough to understand more than she pretends."

"She understands enough to resist."

"She resists because you have always allowed her to believe resistance changes anything."

Viktor's expression did not change, but the room seemed to narrow slightly around the words.

"She is not easy," he said.

"No," Ekaterina agreed. "And she never will be. That is precisely why you should not wait too long to place her well."

Viktor's gaze shifted toward the terrace doors. "You approve of him."

"Yes."

"That quickly."

"No," Ekaterina said. "Not quickly. Correctly."

She closed the seating folder and rested both hands on it.

"He is educated, composed, ambitious without being vulgar about it, and he understands what kind of family this is. He knows how to enter a room. He knows when not to speak. He knows what is at stake."

"And what, exactly, do you think is at stake?"

Ekaterina's expression sharpened slightly. "Do not be theatrical with me, Viktor. You know exactly what is at stake. Juliet is not some second daughter to be married prettily and forgotten. She is our heir."

She paused, then corrected herself.

"She is your heir."

Viktor regarded her but did not answer. He remembered using that same point, and almost that same tone, when speaking to Paris.

Ekaterina continued. "He is not impulsive. He is not stupid. He is not one of those decorative boys who mistake money for strength. He is measured. He will keep her safe."

Viktor's jaw set slightly at that last word.

"Safe," he repeated.

"Yes."

"You say it as if safety has ever been simple."

"No," Ekaterina said. "This family knows all too well that it is neither simple nor assured. The Montagues have taken from us piece by piece—our children, our family, our peace."

For a brief moment, both of their gazes clouded with anger, loss, and regret.

Ekaterina spoke first. "But he is perhaps the best option we have."

Viktor nodded slowly. At the far end of the room, one of the household staff waited with a clipboard in hand, uncertain whether to interrupt. Ekaterina noticed first.

"What is it?"

"The final courier list, madam."

She held out her hand. The staff member crossed the room and passed her the updated invitation list. Ekaterina checked the list once, then noticed an oddity.

"One of these went out late?"

"There was a problem with the delivery service, madam."

Ekaterina's expression did not change. The air still seemed to cool around the answer.

"Did it go?"

"Yes, madam."

"Did we receive a response yet?"

"No, madam. Mr. Mercutio has not responded yet. Should we anticipate him and any guests in the seating chart?"

A brief look of frustration flashed across her face. "Of course. See that nothing else fails."

"Yes, madam."

The staff member inclined his head, turned, and left quickly with the list still in hand. Viktor watched the door close behind him, his mind still caught between being a father and the need to ensure that his family would remain safe and secure long after he himself was only a memory.

Chapter 5. Tuesday Evening — Kapulet Townhouse, Georgetown

Juliet Kapulet hated being dressed for other people's intentions. The gown lay across the chaise in her room, looking less like clothing than a decision someone else had already made for her. Silver-gray silk, narrow through the waist, low across the back, demure enough to satisfy a mother and revealing enough to keep a room looking twice. It had been delivered that morning in a garment bag from a Paris house she had never visited and would never have chosen for herself. On the accompanying card, someone in her mother's office had written only one word in neat black ink: Tonight.

Juliet stood barefoot on the carpet and stared at it as if contempt alone might change the cut. Behind her, Galina moved quietly through the room, laying out earrings, perfume, and shoes with the patient efficiency of a woman who had spent half her life managing crises without comment. She had been Juliet's personal attendant, translator, guardian, and occasional co-conspirator for so long that the official title no longer mattered. In Moscow, she had once been a nurse. In London, she had become Juliet's confidante. In Washington, she had turned into a shadow with opinions.

"It's beautiful," Galina said, which in her voice meant the gown was not to blame for what it had been meant to do.

Juliet folded her arms. "That depends on who has to wear it."

Galina did not smile. She seldom wasted expressions on truths that obvious. "You have worn worse for more annoying people."

"That is not a defense."

"No," Galina said. "It is perspective. Your life is silk and jewels, Juliet. Others are far less fortunate."

Juliet turned from the gown to the long windows overlooking the back garden. Beyond the glass, the winter evening had settled into a dark blue wash over Georgetown. Bare branches scratched faintly against the iron fence. Somewhere below, one of the security men crossed the courtyard and spoke into his wrist mic, his voice lost before it reached the room. The townhouse was taut with preparation—music downstairs, catering staff in motion, her father moving through the rooms like a man checking loaded weapons, her mother arranging the guest list with surgical care. And Juliet, as always, was expected to appear where the evening needed its final polish.

Galina lifted the dress from the chaise and held it up against her. "It will make your mother happy."

"My mother is happiest when I look expensive and quiet."

"Then you should try to do both quickly. She will be here soon."

Juliet closed her eyes briefly. Her mother was never here soon by accident.

"Has she said what this is about?"

Galina took too much care before answering. "She wishes to talk about the winter masquerade."

"It is always a gala or a masquerade. This much, or perhaps this little, silk means there is a man attached."

Galina's mouth twitched at one corner. "Likely."

Juliet turned back. "And you know who he is."

"I know many things."

"Galina."

At that, the older woman relented just enough. "Paris Sokol is expected tonight."

Juliet stayed quiet. She had met Paris twice before: once at a dinner in Vienna, and once in London, where he kissed the back of her hand and spoke briefly. He was handsome, elegant, intelligent, and assembled so carefully by family, schools, and expectation that very little of him seemed accidental. She had disliked him instantly. Not because he was cruel, since cruelty at least had personality. Paris was worse. He was safe and reasonable, which made him harder to dismiss.

"And my father?" she asked.

Galina draped the dress over the back of the chair. "Your father believes Paris is valuable to both family and business interests."

"That was not the question."

"No," Galina agreed. "But it is the answer."

Juliet gave a short exhale through her nose as a knock sounded at the door. Galina and Juliet exchanged a glance.

"See?" Galina said. "Soon."

She crossed the room and opened the door before her mother had to knock again. Juliet's mother entered in a dark green silk blouse and narrow black trousers, every line of her as deliberate as the furniture. She never rushed. Time adjusted itself around Ekaterina Kapulet.

Her gaze moved first to the dress, then to Juliet, then to the untouched tray of tea by the window. "You haven't dressed yet."

Juliet leaned one shoulder against the mantel. "I was admiring the machinery."

Her mother dismissed that with the slightest movement of her hand. "Galina, the earrings are unsuitable."

"They were chosen by your office," Galina said.

"Yes. Which means someone in my office is an idiot. The sapphires."

Galina nodded once and changed them without comment. Her mother walked farther into the room and examined Juliet the way a collector might inspect an auction item. Juliet had inherited her father's height and her mother's composure, which made her easier to display than to direct. From her mother, she had taken her pale complexion, her long blonde hair, and the finer lines of her face.

"Paris will be here tonight," her mother said.

Juliet almost laughed. "Galina already risked state secrets to tell me."

Her mother's expression did not change. "Then she saved me a sentence."

Galina kept her attention fixed on the jewelry. Smart woman.

Ekaterina stopped in front of Juliet. "You will be civil."

"I am always civil."

"Not in the way I mean." Her mother's voice stayed cool, but there was iron beneath it. "You will speak to him for more than two minutes. You will not turn him into sport. You will not punish him for being an aristocrat. He has the drive and the intention to become more than what he was born into."

"That seems unfair," Juliet said. "Why shouldn't he suffer accordingly?"

"Because unlike you, I do not have the luxury of confusing amusement with power. And soon, that luxury will be over. You are twenty-three. Your father's coddling cannot continue forever."

Juliet paused, then turned away before the pause between them hardened into something neither of them could soften. She crossed to the mirror. Her own reflection waited there, pale in the lamplight, blonde hair still loose over one shoulder, face unpainted, expression sharper than the evening required. For a brief, childish second, she considered ruining the whole performance by refusing to dress at all. Then she imagined her father hearing of it downstairs and lost the appetite for it.

"What exactly are his intentions?" she asked at last.

In the mirror, she saw her mother glance once toward Galina, then decide the woman was functionally furniture.

"A future broader than Washington. A future of legitimate business dealings in Europe and here," her mother said. "A future where the Kapulet house does not lose more daughters and sons to violence. A future your father and I very much want to see."

A flood of emotion washed over Juliet—memories, old grief, the keening echo of tear-soaked faces and wailing.

Her mother moved to the dressing table and touched the perfume bottle there, aligning it with the edge of the tray. "This means stability and protection internationally. We have fought for years to legitimize our family. This is the path. You are the key."

"Abroad."

"If necessary."

"Alone."

"You would not be alone," her mother said. "Galina would come. And, in time, children."

Juliet looked over her shoulder at her nurse, at her confidante. There it was beneath the silk and diplomacy: not merely meet him, but prepare to leave. Soon enough to begin taming her resistance in advance. London, perhaps. Geneva. Vienna. Some immaculate apartment above a city she did not love, receiving guests she did not choose, speaking three languages and belonging to none of them. All while her parents called it safety and security, wrapped in the facade of legitimacy.

"What if I say no?" Juliet asked.

Her mother's hands came to rest lightly on the back of the chair. "To conversation?"

"To the arrangement."

Her mother took a moment before answering, which meant the answer mattered. "You are not a foolish girl," she said. "So do not force me to answer a foolish question."

Juliet laughed once. "That bad."

"That simple."

Galina set the sapphire earrings beside the mirror and stepped back. Her face remained neutral, but Juliet knew her well enough to see the tension in her shoulders. She understood this conversation more honestly than her mother did.

"I'm twenty-three," Juliet said.

"Yes."

"Not sixteen."

Her mother met her eyes in the mirror. "No. At sixteen, it was fine for you to believe that defiance by itself could alter an outcome. That is no longer an option."

Juliet sat at the dressing table, her legs weighed down by her mother's words. Emotion rose in her, but she held her tongue. These arguments, civilized as they were, were draining. Galina moved behind her, combing out her hair with careful strokes. The familiarity of it steadied Juliet more than she wanted to admit.

"When did you decide this?" Juliet asked.

"Nothing is decided."

"Then why does it feel that way?"

Her mother bent to fasten one sapphire earring into place herself. Her fingers were cool. "Because you mistake discussion among adults for choice. Whether it is Paris or someone else, the options are limited, and the next prospect will likely not be as good. Paris is handsome, rich, and intelligent. That is more than most women get."

Juliet watched her mother's face in the mirror. Beautiful still. Controlled always. Ekaterina had once terrified rooms simply by entering them, and probably still did. What made her hardest to resist was conviction: she trusted what worked more than what loved her back.

"What if I don't like him?" Juliet asked.

Her mother's expression shifted, not quite into amusement. "Liking him is not a requirement. It is a convenience."

Galina's comb paused, then continued. Juliet stared at herself. There were families in Washington that lied differently from hers. They used therapy language, democratic language, empowerment language. They called control concern and exile opportunity. Under pressure, the language always fell away. Choose correctly. Smile beautifully. Don't embarrass the family. From downstairs came the distant opening phrase of a string quartet warming into its first piece. The guests were arriving.

Her mother straightened. "Dress."

Galina helped Juliet into the gown without speaking. The silk slid cool over her skin. The back fastened with hidden hooks. The waist fit exactly. Of course it did. Someone had taken her measurements more recently than she remembered giving them.

By the time the sapphires were in place and her hair pinned back from one side, Juliet looked like the evening intended her to look: composed, luxurious, faintly untouchable. She hated how well the costume worked. Galina stepped aside, and her mother assessed her daughter.

"There," she said. "You see? No one is imprisoning you."

Juliet met her eyes in the mirror. "No," she said. "Not with iron bars, but with silk."

For the first time all evening, her mother's lips pressed tight with something sharper than impatience. Then it was gone.

"You will come down in five minutes," she said. "Do not make me send for you."

She crossed to the door and opened it.

At the threshold, she stopped and glanced back. "And Juliet—do not confuse resistance with power."

Then she was gone. Galina waited until the door shut fully before speaking.

"You should eat something."

Juliet laughed under her breath. "That is your response?"

"It is always my response when rich and powerful families argue."

Juliet met her eyes in the mirror. "Would you go?"

"If they sent you?"

"Yes."

Galina lifted one shoulder. "Of course."

"And if I didn't want to go?"

Galina's hands settled on the back of the chair. "Then wanting me to go would be the least of your worries."

From below, a murmur of voices swelled, followed by laughter and the chiming notes of crystal touching crystal. Washington in formal wear. Power passing through doorways under soft light. Russian money. Political guests. Shipping interests. Private security. Juliet rose.

Galina reached to smooth one invisible wrinkle near her waist, then touched Juliet once lightly at the shoulder, the gesture almost maternal, almost professional, difficult to separate after all these years.

"You are beautiful," she said. "I have faith in you."

Juliet smiled despite herself. Then she turned and moved toward the door. Toward the music, the guests, Paris Sokol, and the ballroom.

Chapter 6. Tuesday Night — Town Car to the Kapulet Masquerade, Georgetown

Mercutio hated arriving quietly. Even before the car had fully stopped, he had already loosened his bow tie, retied it for the sole purpose of improving the angle, and checked his reflection in the darkened window as if Washington itself might be offended by negligence. Escalus's younger cousin had once been expected to play the good boy in public. Instead, he had turned his good looks into provocation, family disappointment into style, and every formal room in the city into something he entered like a dare.

Benvolio sat opposite him, already regretting every decision that had placed the three of them in the same car. Romeo, tonight, made danger feel like destiny, as if this whole reckless errand were a quest that had to reach its inevitable end. Mercutio only encouraged him, treating the risk like entertainment and his own bad judgment like a form of charm. Benvolio was the opposite of both of them. He trusted exits, sight lines, and the first bad feeling in his stomach. Tonight, that feeling told him they were walking into something none of them could control.

Romeo sat beside the window, one hand loose over his knee, looking out at the row of townhouses sliding past in reflected gold and shadow. He had been quieter since they met back at the car. Not tense, not even nervous; something in him had simply gone still, as if bracing for impact. Mercutio noticed it too. Of course he did. Mercutio noticed everything that might eventually amuse him.

"You look like a man on his way to either a funeral or very bad sex," he said.

Romeo didn't turn from the window. "That's a narrow range of options."

"In this city? Not at all. Sometimes they're the same event."

Benvolio rubbed at the bridge of his nose. "Give me one night without hearing your theories on Washington's moral architecture."

Mercutio smiled. "I don't have theories. I have observations."

"You have a disease."

"Yes," Mercutio said. "Charm."

The town car eased around the corner toward the Kapulet block. The closer they got, the more the neighborhood sharpened into its curated evening self. Townhouses glowed from within like lacquered jewelry boxes. Valets moved briskly beneath streetlamps. Black SUVs idled at the curb with diplomatic plates and tinted windows. Men in tailored coats stood at corners pretending they were not security. Women stepped from cars trailing silk and perfume and the kind of practiced laughter that meant the evening had already begun before they arrived. Mercutio adjusted one cuff and watched Romeo again.

"What's gotten into you?"

Romeo finally turned to him. "Nothing."

"Bad answer."

"It's the only one you're getting."

Mercutio leaned back with a sigh theatrical enough to deserve an audience. "See, this is why I prefer criminals to politicians. Criminals at least admit when they're about to make an interesting mistake."

Benvolio glanced at Romeo. "He has a point."

Romeo gave them both a look that might have passed for irritation if Benvolio hadn't known him so long. "You two are becoming very annoying in concert."

"That's because we care," Mercutio said.

"That's because we're trapped in a moving vehicle," Benvolio corrected.

Mercutio waved him off and turned back to Romeo. "All right. Let's review. We are about to walk into a house full of foreign money, domestic rot, private muscle, public charm, and at least three men who would happily sell each other for a Senate seat and a shipping exemption. Under normal circumstances, I am delighted. Under these circumstances, you look half-embalmed. So I ask again—what's gotten into you?"

Outside, the line of waiting cars slowed to a crawl. A valet opened the door of a silver sedan. A woman in pale blue emerged with a diamond necklace around her throat and the expression of someone already bored by the evening's importance. Beyond her, the Kapulet townhouse rose behind lit windows and black iron like a stage set dressed as permanence.

Then Romeo said, "I had a dream."

Benvolio closed his eyes.

Mercutio's whole face lit up. "Oh, now we're getting somewhere."

"It was a mistake to say anything."

"It was a huge mistake," Mercutio agreed. "But one I appreciate deeply. What kind of dream?"

"The kind I can't shake."

"That's not a kind. That's a complaint."

Romeo looked back out the window. Washington moved in broken reflections across the glass, streetlight over cheekbone, passing headlights over his mouth. "It felt off," he said. "Like the night had already gone bad before it even started."

Mercutio laughed softly, not unkindly. "That's not a dream. That's instinct. Or bad Italian family luck."

"No," Romeo said. "It felt… personal."

The word settled more heavily than the others had. Benvolio watched him in profile. Mercutio did too, though with more curiosity and less caution.

"Personal bad," Mercutio said, "or personal interesting?"

Romeo didn't answer.

Mercutio tipped his head. "Ah. So we're back to very bad sex."

Benvolio muttered, "Christ."

Mercutio ignored him. "Listen to me. Dreams are what happen when the brain gets drunk on its own inventory. Everybody in this city dreams exactly according to appetite. Give a lobbyist six hours of sleep and he'll dream of policy language that launders greed into patriotism. Give a senator a pillow and he'll dream of cameras finding the correct side of his face. Give a man like Viktor Kapulet a soft bed and he'll dream of crude moving through cold water under three flags and two fake registries while no one with a badge can touch him. Give an Italian crime heir a few hours of sleep and he'll dream about his father's empire eating him alive in a better suit."

Romeo's mouth twitched despite himself, and Mercutio saw it. Encouraged, he kept going.

"You know what debutantes dream about in this town?" Mercutio asked. "They dream about marrying the least disgusting source of inherited money within geographic reach. Junior prosecutors dream about righteous headlines. Priests dream about surviving Georgetown without committing a mortal sin. Everybody's dreaming. It doesn't mean anything."

"It means something to the person having it," Benvolio said.

Mercutio pointed at him. "And that is why you will never be invited to the better after-parties."

Benvolio gave him a flat look. "I'm devastated."

Mercutio spread his hands. "My point is simple. Dreams are vanity in costume. The mind puts on a little masque, parades all your appetites through it, and calls itself prophetic because candlelight is flattering."

Romeo said, "You rehearse these speeches, don't you?"

"Never," Mercutio said. "I trust God."

"You don't believe in God."

"I believe He's done extraordinary work with me."

That got a real laugh out of Benvolio, brief and reluctant. Mercutio looked smug for half a second, then leaned forward again, all brightness and cutting edges.

"What exactly happened in this dream?"

Romeo's expression changed, the momentary humor gone before it could leave a mark. He looked down at his hands instead of either of them. "It doesn't matter."

"It mattered enough to bring it up."

"I said it felt off. As if something incredible happened, and something tragic too." Romeo paused. "It is only a dream, as you say."

Mercutio watched him, and this time the teasing softened, though not by much. "All right. Then let's improve the odds. We go in. We smile. We deliver the letter. We leave before somebody's nephew decides honor requires a weapon. Very straightforward."

Benvolio turned his head. "Has anybody ever told you that your definition of straightforward is insane?"

"Frequently. Usually by people boring enough to confuse fear with wisdom."

The car finally came to a stop behind the line of arriving guests. Through the windshield, the Kapulet townhouse glowed in layers—window light, lanterns at the gate, the soft amber wash of uplighting against old brick. Music drifted faintly through the closed car doors, strings and piano and the low hum of gathered wealth. Guests were already moving up the front steps under the eye of security, their masks adding just enough theatricality to make the entire thing feel half diplomatic reception, half pagan rite for the rich. A valet opened the door on Benvolio's side first. Cold air swept in.

Mercutio adjusted his cuffs and straightened. "Masks on, gentlemen. Let's go disappoint our enemies by being prettier than they are."

Benvolio stepped out first, the wind biting at his throat. He buttoned his coat, scanned the entrance, then checked behind him for Romeo. For a moment, Romeo stayed where he was.

He sat in the doorway of the car, one hand still resting against the seat, his gaze fixed not on the house as a whole but somewhere higher up—one of the lit upper windows, perhaps, or the soft spill of movement behind silk curtains. There was no telling. But something in his expression had shifted again. He did not look afraid or cautious. He looked like a man recognizing something before he understood it.

"Romeo," Benvolio said.

Romeo blinked, came back to himself, and stepped out.

"There he is," Mercutio murmured. "For a second I thought the city had taken you personally."

"Maybe it has," Romeo said.

Mercutio grinned. "Excellent. I hate being the only one."

They moved toward the steps. At the curb, another town car discharged a diplomat Benvolio recognized from sanctions briefings and a woman he definitely shouldn't have been seen with in public. A senator from Maryland was already inside. Two embassy aides hovered beneath the awning, pretending not to stare at the guest list. The whole evening reeked of money, leverage, and mutual compromise.

At the top of the steps, one of the Kapulet house managers checked invitations with the kind of neutral politeness that cost decades of training and at least one nervous breakdown. Behind him, security held the line in dark suits and hidden earpieces.

Mercutio handed over his invitation first with a smile that suggested he had never once in his life been denied anything worth having. The house manager checked the card, glanced at each of them in turn, and nodded them through. There was no issue and no delay. Still, Benvolio felt the pressure change the moment they crossed the threshold.

Inside, the entry hall gleamed with old wood, candlelight, marble, and fresh flowers. Footmen took coats. Champagne moved on trays. The air was warmer than outside, heavy with perfume, polished brass, and the faint medicinal edge of security lurking beneath hospitality. From somewhere deeper in the house came music and laughter.

Mercutio accepted a glass of champagne from a passing server and raised it slightly. "To diplomacy," he said. "The last refuge of people who enjoy smiling while they threaten each other."

Benvolio did not take a drink. Romeo took one and held it without tasting it. Guests moved around them in glittering currents. Masks concealed less than they pretended to. A judge's wife. An energy consultant. A member of the Foreign Relations Committee. A lobbyist with three open investigations and the confidence of a man who knew none of them would matter. Washington with its face powdered and its hands hidden.

Mercutio leaned closer to Benvolio. "Where's Tybalt?"

"Not here yet," Benvolio said.

"Pity. He usually improves a room by giving it drama."

But Benvolio had already stopped listening. Because across the far side of the ballroom, beyond the chandeliers, mirrored panels, and drifting clusters of people, movement at the top of the staircase drew the room's attention in a single quiet shift. A woman had appeared there in silver-gray silk.

Benvolio saw only the outline first—poised against light, pale skin, blonde hair swept back from one side, one hand resting lightly on the banister. Then the room parted around her beauty. Juliet Kapulet descended the staircase.

Mercutio noticed the same second and let out the softest whistle. "Well," he said. "At last, the room improves."

Benvolio turned. Romeo had gone utterly still. Not like a man surprised. Like a man struck. He stood with the untouched champagne glass loose in one hand and his gaze fixed upward with such complete and reckless attention that, for an instant, Benvolio felt the whole room tilt around it. Everything else—the music, the guests, the politics, the money, the criminal business beneath all that polish—fell away from Romeo's face so thoroughly it was almost frightening to witness. Juliet reached the last step. She turned her head slightly, scanning the room in the automatic, careful way of someone raised under observation. And then she saw him.

The distance between them was too great for speech, too crowded for movement, but Benvolio felt the collision anyway. It was there in the way her expression sharpened into awareness.

Benvolio looked from one to the other and said, "Oh, that's bad."

Mercutio didn't immediately answer. Instead, a grin started to appear on his face. Across the ballroom, Juliet Kapulet stood in silver and sapphires beneath the lights of her father's house. Near the entrance, Romeo Montague watched her without blinking.

Chapter 7. Tuesday Night — Ballroom, Kapulet Townhouse, Georgetown

The ballroom had been arranged to make excess look effortless. Crystal and candlelight warmed the high ceilings, though the house itself still carried a Georgetown atmosphere beneath all the gold—old brick, dark wood, history repurposed by money. A string quartet played from the far alcove, the music drifting over conversation without ever drowning it. Waiters moved through the room with champagne and caviar blinis, faces neutral, steps exact. Everywhere Romeo looked, there were masks, jewels, polished shoes, low laughter, and the particular alertness of people who had come to enjoy themselves without ever forgetting what it cost to be there.

He had been in rooms like this before. He knew the choreography. Smile just enough. Listen more than speak. Let other people reveal themselves by filling quiet spaces. Watch the hands instead of the mouths. Note who entered together, who did not acknowledge each other too quickly, who drank too fast, who barely touched the glass they carried. In another life, perhaps, it might even have been entertaining. Tonight it all felt unreal. Because every time he tried to look anywhere else, his gaze found its way back to Juliet Kapulet.

She was moving through the ballroom now as if she belonged to it and hated it equally, which somehow made her more striking than the women who had dressed for conquest. The silver-gray gown caught the light and refused to hold it. The sapphires at her ears flashed when she turned her head. Men watched her because men with power always watched beauty as if they desired to claim it. Women watched her too, with that sharper look women reserved for one another.

Romeo stood near a marble column with Benvolio to one side and Mercutio to the other, aware that both of them had noticed the way he had gone still.

"Try not to look like you've been shot," Mercutio murmured into his champagne.

Romeo kept his eyes on Juliet. "Is it that obvious?"

"To us? Completely." Mercutio took a drink. "To everyone else, maybe you can still pass for a man having a very intense thought about dock access and union politics."

Benvolio's voice was lower, more cautious. "Romeo."

He heard the warning in it without needing it explained. Be smart. Stay on task. Do not let a beautiful woman in a rival house own you. Too late.

Across the room, Viktor Kapulet had stopped near the fireplace with Paris Sokol at his side. Paris bent toward Juliet as she reached the edge of their circle and said something meant, presumably, to pass for charm. She listened. Then she smiled with polite restraint, and Romeo, absurdly, hated him.

Mercutio followed his line of sight and gave a soft click of his tongue. "Ah. There he is. The man her mother would place beside her in every photograph—Washington's most eligible bachelor, Paris Sokol, billionaire aristocrat."

"He's not her husband. Yet," Romeo said.

Mercutio raised one eyebrow. "Why should you care what they are or are not?"

Benvolio exhaled quietly. "This is exactly what I was worried about."

Mercutio laughed under his breath. "No, it isn't. You were worried we'd be found out and thrown out if we were lucky, stuffed into several trash bags if we were not."

Benvolio nodded once. "Yes, that too. But this is not a good start to the night."

Mercutio grinned. "No, but it is fascinating. I actually feel quite lively. This is already more entertaining than I hoped."

Benvolio rolled his eyes so forcefully it looked painful. "I am going to die. You are literally going to get me killed."

Mercutio lifted his glass slightly. "Perhaps."

At the far end of the ballroom, a burst of laughter rose near the musicians as a tray of glasses nearly tipped and was saved at the last second by a footman moving faster than he looked capable of moving. Heads turned. Voices lifted. For a brief moment, the attention of the room dispersed, scattering into smaller currents. In that small break, Juliet glanced away from Paris—and found Romeo again. This time, the look held.

She did not know who he was. Not fully. He wore a black mask cut close to the face, clean enough to conceal him without turning him theatrical. He had unusual restraint for a room like this. Most men here performed ease. He seemed to have forgotten performance entirely. Even from across the ballroom, she could feel the directness of his attention, and it struck her with such force that, for one instant, she forgot Paris's voice, her mother's instructions, and the exact place she was supposed to be standing. Then someone spoke to her and the spell broke. But not completely.

Juliet turned her face back toward Paris and heard nothing he said for the next several seconds. Some foolish, disobedient part of her had already gone elsewhere. The first dance began with the sort of formal grace only rich people still believed looked natural.

The quartet shifted into a brighter piece. A space opened in the center of the room. Older guests stepped back. Younger ones moved in. Paris offered Juliet his hand with practiced confidence, and because refusing him in front of half the city would have caused exactly the kind of scene her mother had warned against, Juliet placed her fingers in his.

He was a competent dancer. Of course he was. His hand was warm, his smile measured, his steps perfectly judged to make a woman feel guided rather than measured. He asked polite questions. He commented on the guest list. He spoke of Washington as if it were an amusing inconvenience and Europe as if it remained the last place taste had survived. Juliet answered where she had to. But over Paris's shoulder, beyond the moving bodies and candlelight, she could still see the stranger in black watching her.

It was not merely that he was handsome, though he was. Strong lines made softer by the shadow of the mask. Dark hair. Mouth too serious for the room. It was the sense of withheld motion about him, as if he were only barely choosing to remain where he stood. Men usually looked at her in ways she understood. Desire. Vanity. Curiosity. This felt different.

When the dance turned and Paris guided her into a slow crossing step, Juliet let her gaze stray one second longer than she should have. The stranger had moved closer. Not enough for passing guests to notice. Enough for a careful observer.

"You seem distracted," Paris said.

Juliet brought her attention back to him. "Do I?"

He smiled. "Slightly. I'm choosing not to be wounded."

"How generous."

He accepted the coolness of that with admirable composure. "You may not believe this, Juliet, but I came prepared to earn a difficult evening."

"There are easier ways to damage your self-esteem."

"And less efficient ones."

She almost laughed, which annoyed her.

Then Paris faced her more directly and said, "You look as if you would rather be anywhere else."

Juliet did not bother to deny it. "Would you prefer I lie?"

"No," he said. "I prefer honesty—brutal honesty in private conversation. But in public, you must learn to mask your emotions, lest others use them against you."

Juliet's eyes narrowed. "Are you able to put your emotions away so easily?"

"Yes," he said. "And if we are to have any future together, you will need to learn to do the same."

At the edge of the dance floor, Ekaterina stood beside a senator's wife, smiling with the serene confidence of a woman whose daughter was doing exactly what was required of her. Viktor, a little farther off, was deep in conversation with a former ambassador but watched the room without appearing to. Nothing in this house happened unwitnessed for long. Juliet completed the turn, separated from Paris for a brief space, then returned to him for the next movement.

By the time the music ended, Juliet had decided two things. Paris Sokol was exactly as frightening as she had feared, not because he was monstrous, but because he could make a cage look like a fairy tale. He was handsome enough, civilized enough, and strategic enough that everyone around her would call it fortune while she slowly vanished inside it. The stranger in black felt like the opposite of that, though Juliet did not yet know whether that made him salvation or another kind of ruin. Already, he was a temptation that made her pulse quicken and her judgment falter.

Paris bowed slightly as the final note faded. "May I bring you something to drink?"

"You may bring me distance," she said with a polite and generous smile.

To his credit, he smiled back. "I'll take that as progress."

He stepped away neither pleased nor discouraged, and that more than anything made her wary. Juliet watched him go and became aware that someone else had taken the place he had left open.

"Harsh," a male voice said near her shoulder.

She turned. The stranger stood close enough now that she could see his eyes clearly through the mask. They were darker than she had thought from across the room, steady and intent and entirely too interested for a first meeting.

"That depends," Juliet said, "on whether he deserved mercy."

"He looked rich enough to survive disappointment."

"He'll be relieved to hear it."

A faint smile touched his mouth. Up close, he was taller than she had judged, broader through the shoulders, his black evening clothes fitting with the kind of precision that suggested either old money or crime money refined by a very good tailor. Nothing about him was showy. That was part of why he stood out.

He held out a fresh champagne flute taken from a passing tray. "Peace offering?"

Juliet considered the glass, then him. "For what offense?"

"For overhearing enough to admire your performance."

She took the drink. "Then you're rewarding bad behavior."

"I'm encouraging good taste."

It didn't sound rehearsed.

"Are you one of my father's guests," she asked, "or one of the people who follow them in hoping for better alcohol?"

"I was invited."

"That's not an answer."

"It's the safest one available."

There was humor in his voice, yes, but also caution—as if names mattered here in a way they didn't for most people in the room.

Juliet lifted the glass without drinking. "You're mysterious."

"No," he said. "Just trained."

Juliet did not smile.

Her gaze narrowed just enough to interest him. "Trained for what?"

"Bad parties."

This time she laughed, quick and unwilling, and the sound altered his face. Around them, the ballroom kept moving. Another set of guests entered. A server drifted by with silver trays. Near the fireplace, Viktor turned slightly, speaking to the ambassador while scanning the room. Ekaterina had shifted farther toward the musicians. Benvolio, at the room's edge, watched Romeo with the expression of a man witnessing a slow-motion structural failure. Mercutio watched too, but he looked delighted.

Juliet could feel how precarious this was. Nothing improper had happened, yet she was already standing too long with a stranger whose attention she should not enjoy.

"Do you always stare at women from across crowded rooms?" she asked.

"Only when they make it difficult not to."

This man regarded her and simply meant it. Juliet took her first sip of champagne to buy herself a second.

"You're either very bold," she said, "or very foolish."

He tilted his head. "Those aren't mutually exclusive."

"No," she said. "They rarely are."

The music shifted again, slower now. More intimate. The space between one dance and the next thinned as couples rearranged themselves. He extended his hand, and Juliet stared at it. He did not say dance with me. The offer rested there between them, graceful in its simplicity. Her first instinct was refusal; her second, more treacherous instinct, was to see what would happen if she said yes. So she put her hand in his. His fingers closed around hers with restrained warmth, and the contact sent a clean shock through her. He led her onto the floor.

He was a better dancer than Paris—not technically, perhaps, but more naturally. Paris guided by formula. This man adapted. Juliet should have disliked that. Instead, she found herself looking up at him through the shifting light and wondering what the rest of his face looked like without the mask.

"You still haven't told me who you are," she said.

"Reason says I shouldn't."

That sharpened her interest more than a smoother answer would have.

"Reason is rarely invited to dances like this," she said.

"No," he said. "But it survives them longer."

A hint of a smile touched her mouth. "So you do have some."

"Enough to know I came into this house carrying something meant for you."

Juliet's head tilted slightly. "Something meant for me?"

"Yes."

"And yet you won't tell me who you are."

"If I tell you too soon, your cousin will hear it before it does either of us any good."

That, more than the caution in his voice, told her he already knew exactly where he was and who she belonged to.

"Then why come at all?" she asked.

He held her gaze one suspended instant too long.

"Because I knew who you were the moment I saw you," he said quietly. "I just didn't realize…"

He stopped.

Juliet faltered despite herself. "Didn't realize what?"

His gaze moved over her face with a kind of startled sincerity she had not expected to find in this room, or in any man sent toward her by design.

"I didn't realize you were this beautiful."

A faint flush rose into her cheeks before she could stop it. Not because she had never heard the word before. Men had been handing it to her all her life like tribute. But those compliments usually came wrapped in appetite, polish, or strategy. This was something else. It was plain enough to make her feel seen rather than admired. He saw it. His expression altered, not into triumph, but into something softer and more astonished.

"You see?" she said, recovering just enough to make the line edged. "That sounds less like caution than a very poorly disguised advance."

"It was not meant to be," he said. "But it certainly is."

"That," Juliet said, "is interesting."

His gaze dropped to her, and a hint of a smile appeared.

"You still haven't told me who you are," she said again.

"I was enjoying the advantage while I had it."

"So you admit there is one."

"Yes," he said. "I believe you're right."

She smiled mischievously. He drew her through the turn, and for one suspended moment, the room seemed to thin around them. The chandeliers blurred. The music softened. Her hand rested against his shoulder; his palm held the shape of her waist with infuriating certainty.

"Tell me something else," Romeo asked.

"Such as?"

"Whether you hate this as much as it looks like you do."

Juliet faltered.

Her answer came before caution could intervene. "More."

His mouth changed, not fully into a smile, but close enough to make warmth move through her too quickly.

"I thought so."

"You say that as if you know me."

"No," he said. "I say it as if I want to."

Around them, other couples kept moving, but Juliet had abruptly become aware of how little distance remained. At the edge of the room, Tybalt had appeared. He stopped near one of the columns, accepted a drink he did not want, and lifted his gaze toward the dance floor.

At first, he only saw Juliet. That was natural. Rooms did that around her. His eyes followed the turn of her body through the slower measure of the dance, and only then did he register the man holding her. Not Paris.

That caught his attention first. Paris he understood, or thought he did—polish, breeding, measured ambition, the kind of man mothers approved of because sophistication disguised appetite more cleanly than brutality ever could. This stranger was something else. Black mask. Dark evening clothes.

Stillness without weakness. Control without submission. Tybalt had spent his life sorting rooms into wolves and sheep, and this man did not belong among the sheep. Tybalt watched another turn.

The man bent his head and said something to Juliet. Tybalt did not catch the words. He did not need to. The voice carried just enough across the music to trouble him. He frowned.

Not because he knew it at once, but because something in it had settled where memory lived. He kept watching. The next turn gave him more: the line of the shoulders beneath the coat, the height, the deliberate economy of his movements, the way he held Juliet not like a social climber dazzled by proximity, but like a man already too certain of himself to perform awe for the room. Another few quiet words passed between them. Tybalt heard the voice again. This time, his eyes widened.

He had seen Romeo Montague in person before—at the courthouse, at one donor event his mother had insisted he attend, and once across a restaurant room where both families pretended not to recognize each other. But it was not the face that fixed it. The mask denied him that. It was the voice first, and then the bearing, the movement, the insolent familiarity of him. Everything else fell into place. Across the room, Benvolio saw it happen and felt his stomach drop.

Mercutio followed his gaze. "Ah," he said under his breath, with a mix of sadness and excitement. "We're moving into the climax already?"

Tybalt began moving. On the dance floor, Romeo had not seen him yet. Juliet had. The instant she caught Tybalt's expression, every childhood instinct she had lit at once. The danger was immediate. She returned her attention to the man holding her.

"Don't turn around," she said.

He felt it in her voice and obeyed. "Why?"

"My cousin is coming this way."

Readiness flashed through him.

"The one who looks like murder in a coat?" he asked.

Against all reason, Juliet nearly laughed. "Yes."

"Should I be flattered?"

"No. You should be gone."

But Tybalt was already too close for a clean retreat. He came to the edge of the dance floor with lethal calm, every inch of him restrained now in the way that usually meant violence had moved from possibility into inevitability. He waited until the turn of the dance brought Romeo and Juliet nearer, then spoke just loudly enough for the people closest to hear.

"I know that voice."

Romeo turned then.

Tybalt's gaze locked on him, and contempt flashed hot and bright through the polish. "Montague."

Juliet felt Romeo's hand tighten once at her waist. Not forcefully, just enough to tell her he understood. Several nearby couples slowed. Conversation at the nearest cluster dimmed. Across the room, Viktor saw Tybalt's face and began crossing toward them.

Romeo let Juliet's hand go carefully. "You're mistaken."

Tybalt smiled without humor. "No. I never am."

The ballroom had not yet fully stopped, but it was close. The string quartet faltered, recovered, and kept playing because musicians in rooms like this knew that social collapse, like weather, was not reason to interrupt the program unless injury made it unavoidable. Tybalt stepped closer. Juliet moved before she thought better of it. She caught his sleeve.

"Don't," she said in Russian, low and cutting.

He didn't take his eyes off Romeo. "Move."

"Not here."

"Then he should not have come here."

Viktor reached them a heartbeat later. "Tybalt."

The single word landed with more force than a shout would have. Tybalt turned toward him. That was all Viktor needed.

"What are you doing?" Viktor asked.

The question was mild, which meant everyone listening understood it as a warning.

Tybalt gestured once toward Romeo. "A Montague in our house."

Viktor's gaze moved over Romeo. It lingered only a second, but in that second, Juliet felt the whole night go tense. Then Viktor smiled. It was a public smile. Diplomatic and harmless on the surface, more menacing than Tybalt with a blade.

"And yet," Viktor said, "he seems to be behaving better than family."

A ripple of nervous laughter moved through the nearest guests. Just enough to ease the immediate tension. Just enough to preserve appearances.

Tybalt stared at him, disbelieving. "You would let him stand here?"

"I would not have a scene made in my house because my nephew confuses temper with authority." Viktor's voice stayed soft. "If he has been invited, he is a guest. If he is a guest, he will be treated as one."

Tybalt's expression hardened. Juliet knew that look. Submission, for the moment only, with the insult stored for later.

Viktor turned to Romeo now, every inch the gracious host. "Washington is a small city," he said. "These things happen. Enjoy the evening."

The message beneath the words was clear enough. You have been seen. You remain only because I allow it.

Romeo inclined his head. "Of course."

Tybalt gave him one last look, all promise and poison, then stepped back. Galina appeared beside Juliet as if she had materialized from the watching crowd. She placed a hand lightly at Juliet's elbow—not enough to drag, but enough to claim her attention.

"You're wanted by the ambassador's wife," Galina said.

Juliet understood at once. She was being removed from the center of the room before scandal could thicken, and Galina had chosen the excuse before anyone else thought to use force. She glanced at Romeo one final time before allowing Galina to guide her away. He was watching her with that same unwavering focus. For one reckless instant, she wished the room would catch fire. Then she was gone into the crowd.

Chapter 8. Tuesday Late Night — Ballroom and Side Corridor, Kapulet Townhouse, Georgetown

The party recovered because parties like this always did. Wealth had no greater talent than stepping over fresh tension to refill its glass. Mercutio joined Romeo near the side corridor before Benvolio could get there first.

"Well," Mercutio said, "that went better than expected."

Benvolio came up on his other side. "Don't encourage him. We're not out of this yet, and all we did was paint a target on our heads."

"I'm not encouraging him. I'm reassessing our odds."

Romeo barely heard them. His eyes were still searching the room.

"You need to leave," Benvolio said.

"Not yet."

"Romeo."

He turned then, just enough for Benvolio to see the change in him clearly. The earlier restlessness from that morning was gone. But rather than calming him, the change made him look determined and focused.

"No," Romeo said. "Not yet."

Before Benvolio could answer, a side door opened farther down the corridor. Galina stepped through first. She emerged half-shadowed by the doorway, one hand still on the brass handle, her gaze moving over the corridor with quiet precision. She looked first toward the ballroom, then toward Benvolio and Mercutio, then finally at Romeo. Nothing in her expression changed, but something in her attention sharpened. Only then did Juliet appear behind her.

For a brief second, Juliet remained in the doorway, listening for pursuit. Whatever excuse had separated her from the ballroom had worked, but not for long. She was breathing slightly faster than she should have been. A loose strand of blonde hair had fallen near her temple. She saw Romeo. Neither Benvolio nor Mercutio moved. Juliet started toward him, but Galina moved first.

Not quickly. Not dramatically. Just one smooth step into Romeo's path, close enough to stop him without ever touching him. She gave him an appraising look—the suit, the mask, the posture, the way his attention had already gone past her to Juliet.

"You are Romeo Montague," Galina said quietly, out of Juliet's earshot.

Romeo held her gaze. "Yes."

"I know."

The words carried no surprise. Only judgment.

Juliet said, "Galina—"

Galina lifted one hand without looking back. "No. A man bold enough to enter this house may survive one warning."

Mercutio's mouth curved faintly. Benvolio did not look amused at all. Galina stepped closer to Romeo and lowered her voice further, so the threat belonged only to him.

"If you hurt her," she said, "if you make yourself one more man who mistakes her courage for permission to be careless, I will not wait for her father, her mother, or her cousin to punish you."

Romeo did not look away.

"I understand."

"No," Galina said. "You hear me. Understanding and regret come later."

For a suspended moment, the corridor held still around them. Then Galina stepped aside. Juliet crossed the corridor toward Romeo with measured speed, every line of her body saying she understood exactly how reckless it was to be there and had chosen it anyway. When she stopped in front of him, the air between them felt charged enough to strike.

"You should have left," she said.

"So should you."

Somewhere behind the door Juliet had come through, voices rose and receded. The ballroom remained only one door away, but here the light was lower, warmer, the sounds of the party softened by walls and distance. Juliet glanced once past Romeo—at Benvolio, at Mercutio, at Galina, at the corridor—and lowered her voice.

"Not here."

She turned slightly and pushed open the narrow door beside her, the one leading into a small adjoining sitting room.

Benvolio stepped forward at once. "Absolutely not."

Mercutio caught his sleeve before he could interfere. "Oh, let them at least conduct the disaster in private."

Galina gave him a look cutting enough to take the shine off his smile.

"You are children," she said to Mercutio and Benvolio.

Mercutio blinked. "Madam, I have been accused of many things, but rarely youth."

"Foolish children," Galina corrected.

Juliet was already inside. Romeo started to follow, but Galina caught his sleeve lightly. He stopped.

"You have minutes," she said. "Not destiny. Not permission. Minutes."

Romeo nodded once. Galina released him. He followed Juliet into the sitting room. Benvolio swore under his breath and positioned himself by the door, back to the wood, watching the corridor. Mercutio took up the opposite side with visible delight and lifted his champagne like a man settling in for theater.

Inside, the room was small and dimly lit, more a private withdrawing room than a formal salon. A pair of gilt chairs sat near the wall. A lamp burned low on a side table. The sounds of the ballroom came through softened now—music, laughter, the drift of moneyed conversation blurred into atmosphere. Juliet turned to face him.

"I know you are a Montague," she said. "But who are you exactly?"

"Did she not tell you?" Romeo asked.

"Galina?" Juliet asked. "No, we really haven't had a chance to talk. Who are you? Be straight with me."

"Romeo," he said, flatly.

Juliet's eyes widened slightly. "Romeo Montague."

He did not deny it.

She gave an exhale that was almost a laugh, though there was no humor in it. "Of course. But what is in a name, after all? If I called you something else, would it change who you are—or how I feel standing here?"

"How you feel?" Romeo asked, a taste of wanting in his voice.

A smile quirked on her face. "Oh, Romeo, who you are and the very sight of you stir up things in me I do not know how to describe. You are mysterious, bold, and intense. You intrigue me, but you scare me too."

"As do you," he said, locking eyes with her. Then, after the briefest hesitation, he continued more quietly, "But honestly, I did not come to make trouble for you or your family. I apologize for that. Truly. But in my heart, I am glad that I came, if it meant I would see you."

Juliet's eyes lowered. "Then why did you come?"

Before he could lose the nerve for honesty, Romeo reached inside his coat and drew out the envelope he had carried every day since the tragedy. Juliet Kapulet was written across the front in Rosaline's hand, and the back was closed with an old-fashioned wax seal.

"I brought something from Rosaline."

"Rosaline?" Juliet's voice changed at once. "I heard the terrible news. But how do you know Rosaline?"

"We were lovers," he said, sadness and regret roughening the words. "I was with her when she died. We were driving to deliver this letter from her to you."

Juliet stared at the letter. "We weren't speaking."

"I know."

"How could you know that?"

"Because she told me she wanted to make amends to some broken friendship." He held the letter out. "I do not know what she wrote. I did not open it. Nor did she tell me why your friendship ended. All I know is that this was incredibly important to her, and I wanted to make sure it reached you, because after she died, it became important to me too."

Juliet took the letter slowly, almost against her own will.

"Tybalt would have burned it," she said after a moment.

"I feared the same thing, and I could not chance it."

Her fingers tightened once around the envelope. When she looked up again, something in her expression had shifted.

"You came into my father's house to deliver Rosaline's apology."

"Yes."

"That is either very kind or very stupid."

"It's been a mixed evening."

Romeo edged closer to her. Not enough to touch her. Enough that when Juliet looked down at the worn envelope and saw the familiar shape of Rosaline's handwriting, the feeling hit before she could stop it. Emotion caught in her throat with a gasp. Tears welled. Her shoulders softened all at once under the weight of it. Romeo moved without thinking and folded his arms around her. It was not seduction. Not strategy. Only a human embrace offered to another human already breaking.

At first, Juliet remained stiff with surprise. Then she sagged against him, clutching the letter in one hand while the other found the front of his coat. Her forehead came to rest against his chest. He felt the tremor in her breath, the small helpless sounds she tried and failed to contain, and held her as if there were any use in that at all. They stood that way longer than either of them should have, long enough for their emotions to change shape.

His warm scent and her perfume mingled in the narrow room. The warmth of their bodies met and steadied. Slowly, almost without deciding to, they loosened their hold on each other just enough. She tilted her face toward his.

He lowered his. They were still in each other's arms when the kiss happened. Not lust. Not grief. Something stranger than both. Something that felt less chosen than yielded to.

The kiss landed softly, then deepened, as if restraint had only been a courtesy neither of them had ever truly intended to keep. The taste of champagne still lingered faintly on her lips. His hand came to the side of her face, careful and unsteady. She rose slightly into him, fingers finding the front of his coat, and for one suspended, reckless moment, the whole world reduced itself to warmth and the sudden relief of contact honestly wanted. When they broke apart, neither of them moved far.

Juliet's voice was lower now, roughened in a way that sent heat through him. "That was a mistake."

"Probably."

"We shouldn't have done that."

"And yet, we did."

A swell of voices rose in the corridor outside. Then footsteps, nearer now. Someone laughed too loudly. Somewhere beyond that, a sharper voice called for Juliet from deeper in the ballroom. Both of them snapped back half a step.

Juliet glanced toward the door, then back to him. Her expression had changed. Softer, yes. But not safe. Harder to deny, if anything, because now they had crossed from fascination into knowledge.

"I have to go."

"When will I see you again?" he asked.

Juliet's mouth nearly curved, but sadness touched it before it formed. "You shouldn't."

"And yet I want to."

The sounds outside sharpened again—movement, voices, the machinery of the house drawing near.

Juliet backed toward the door. "Then you'll have to be more clever than that, Romeo Montague, if you wish to see me again."

She slipped out first, with Galina stepping to her side. Mercutio straightened from the wall as she passed, his expression instantly wiped clean of amusement into something that could almost pass for decorous neutrality. Benvolio gave her one quick, searching look, then stepped aside without a word. Juliet went back toward the ballroom with the letter clutched lightly in her hand. A second later, Benvolio opened the door and went inside. Mercutio followed at once. Romeo was still standing where Juliet had left him.

"This," Benvolio said, "is exactly how careers and lives get destroyed."

Romeo turned toward the door she had just gone through and said, "Noted."

Mercutio arrived at Benvolio's shoulder, drinking from a new champagne glass. "On the other hand," he said, "if one is going to be destroyed, this is an excellent start to a story."

Benvolio stared at him. "I need you to be less happy."

"No," Mercutio said. "You need me to be exactly this happy, because one of us should appreciate the story that is unfolding before us. It is truly epic."

Across the ballroom, Juliet had already returned to the crowd. Ekaterina was speaking to her. Paris stood somewhere to her left. Viktor remained near the fireplace, one hand in his pocket, watching the room with his usual measured patience. Tybalt was no longer visible. The evening—and his life—had changed, and Romeo knew it.

Chapter 9. Tuesday Late Night — Outside the Kapulet Townhouse, Georgetown

The party spilled into the cold in waves of black coats, hired cars, and diplomatic laughter already flattening into fatigue. By the time Romeo reached the front steps with Benvolio and Mercutio, the chandeliers behind them had softened to a distant gold through the glass, and Georgetown had gone dark and cold again—wet brick, bare branches, wind funneling between townhouses with enough force to make every departing guest hunch at the shoulders. Valets were still running. Security still held the line. The string quartet, muffled now by walls and distance, sounded like something being remembered badly.

"Well," Mercutio said, "that was excellent. Threats, foreign money, and at least one morally unsound kiss. I call that a success."

Romeo's head whipped toward him. "How do you know about the kiss?"

Mercutio laughed. "I didn't know for sure until just now. But the way you two looked at each other was a clue, and the faint smear of makeup on your shirt and jacket helped."

Benvolio shot him a look. "Romeo, do you truly have a death wish?"

Romeo stopped at the curb and turned once toward the townhouse the way a man turns toward something he has already left badly once and knows, with fresh disgust, he is about to leave badly again. Benvolio saw it.

"Don't," he said.

Romeo kept his eyes on the house. "Don't what?"

"Whatever you're thinking."

"I'm not thinking anything."

Mercutio glanced between them and gestured to Romeo. "That is obviously untrue. Romeo here looks like a man halfway between revelation and felony."

Benvolio stepped closer. "Listen to me. You got out clean. Tybalt didn't get what he wanted. Viktor played host instead of executioner. That is the best possible version of tonight. Don't ruin it because you suddenly think the laws of human disaster don't apply to you."

The cold had sharpened Romeo's face. He looked different from the man who had arrived at the masquerade—not calmer, exactly, but fixed now around a point that had not existed before. Benvolio had seen obsession take root before. Cases. Revenge. Duty sharpened into identity. But this was stranger, more intimate, and infinitely worse because some part of Romeo already knew it.

"I'm not ruining anything," Romeo said.

Benvolio opened the rear passenger door and jerked his head toward the car. "Get in."

Romeo looked once more at the house. Then the first shot cracked across the night from the rear of the property. The sound ricocheted down the block with enough force to stop conversation mid-breath. A second shot followed, then glass breaking somewhere behind the townhouse, then the ugly, rapid bloom of yelling from inside the house. Italian. Fast, clipped, and too loud to be accidental.

One of the valets dropped a tray of keys. The nearest security men turned as one toward the side alley, hands inside coats, radios erupting alive. The front entrance of the townhouse slammed inward as someone inside shouted for the doors to be locked.

Benvolio grabbed Romeo's sleeve. "In the car."

Romeo tore free.

"Romeo—"

But he was already moving—past the street, past safety, back toward the house. The front doors were being sealed. The visible security had pivoted toward the side access, leaving the garden path briefly unsecured. Romeo cut across the iron fence line, vaulted the low stone lip of the neighboring yard, and ran along the narrow strip of winter grass toward the rear gate. He heard Benvolio behind him, heard Mercutio somewhere farther back saying something profane and bright with disbelief, but the noise inside the house had already overtaken all of it. The rear service door stood half-open, swinging on one hinge in the wind.

One of the Kapulet guards came backward through it, weapon up, face turned toward the interior. Then two shots cracked from inside the service corridor. The guard jerked once and went down heavily on the brick. Romeo dropped behind the low garden wall as the Italian voices surged closer.

"Muoviti. La ragazza."

The girl. His stomach went cold. Inside, the service corridor beyond the kitchen was chaos: staff running, security pushing inward, smoke hanging low from shattered fixtures, somebody calling for Viktor, somebody else shouting that Montague men had breached the rear line. Montague. The word cut through the house with more force than the gunfire. Romeo froze for half a second. Not because it was true, but because it was exactly the kind of lie that could get everyone killed before truth caught up. He moved low through the rear service door. Near the side corridor leading toward the wine level, Galina had Juliet behind her. Not beside her, but behind her.

The older woman had one arm forced back across Juliet's waist, pushing her into the protection of the wall, while her other hand held a small kitchen knife taken from somewhere in the chaos. Her expression had changed completely. The quiet servant, nurse, guardian, and shadow was gone. What remained was older, harder, and far more lethal. A second Kapulet security man stepped in front of them, firing twice toward the pantry entrance. The answering shots came immediately. He went down under them, crashing into the sideboard and dragging a tray of glasses with him. Juliet flinched, but Galina did not.

She shoved Juliet lower and kicked the fallen guard's weapon away from the open corridor with a precision that did not belong to panic. Then one of the attackers came through the smoke.

Dark tactical clothing. No insignia. Mask half torn loose. Italian curses under his breath. He moved fast, too fast for a household guard and too disciplined for a drunk street-level thug. His pistol swung toward Galina first. Galina caught Juliet by the shoulder and threw her aside with enough force to save her from the shot. The round shattered the mirror behind them. Glass exploded across the corridor. Juliet cried out as one bright edge grazed her temple.

Galina struck the attacker's wrist with the knife hand, not stabbing, but redirecting. The next shot went into the ceiling. The attacker snarled and drove forward, catching Galina by the arm and twisting with enough force to wrench the knife from her hand. Juliet lunged for it. The attacker saw her move and seized her by the wrist before she could reach the blade. Romeo hit him from the side.

The force drove the attacker, Romeo, and Juliet into the wall. The attacker's pistol skidded across the floor. Romeo caught fabric, shoulder, bone. Somebody's elbow struck him in the mouth. He tasted copper. The attacker twisted under him with trained violence and reached for a blade at his belt. Juliet saw it first.

"Romeo!"

She kicked the attacker's wrist before the knife came free. The blade clattered once against the floor. Romeo got there first. The attacker slammed a knee into Romeo's ribs with enough force to knock the breath from him. Romeo caught the man by the collar, drove him backward into the broken sideboard, then seized the knife and turned with the motion. The blade went in under the attacker's ribs. Not clean, not graceful, but necessary. The man made a short, shocked sound and folded against Romeo's shoulder before dropping to the floor. Nobody moved.

Then Galina was there, the attacker's pistol in her hand, and behind her lay two other attackers on the floor. Galina grabbed Juliet first, checking her face, her arms, the cut at her temple. Then she turned to Romeo, at the split in his mouth, the torn shoulder of his coat, the blood on his hand where the knife had cut him before it changed owners.

"You," she said, voice low and furious. "Can you move?"

Romeo nodded once.

"I need you to answer me," Galina said, concerned that Romeo was disoriented.

"Yes," he said, regaining his voice.

Another Italian voice shouted from the kitchen side. Galina turned toward it, listening. There was no fear in her face.

She seized Juliet's wrist and shoved her toward the cellar stairs. "Down."

Juliet resisted. "Galina—"

"Down," she ordered.

The command had enough force in it that even Romeo obeyed. Galina pushed them both toward the cellar door and stairs, one hand on Juliet's back.

"You lock this door from the inside," she said. "You do not open it unless you hear my voice. Not a guard's voice. Not even your father's. Mine."

Romeo glanced over his shoulder. "What are you going to do?"

"Give them something else to chase."

Juliet's face went white. "No."

Galina's expression softened for half a second, no longer than that. "Yes."

Then she shoved Juliet through the door and faced Romeo.

"And you," she said, "keep her alive."

Romeo held her gaze. "I will."

"I know you will."

Then Galina slammed the cellar door between them. Romeo threw the iron slide across just as something heavy struck the far end of the corridor above. Galina's voice rose, cutting and commanding, in Italian this time.

"Di qua! She went this way!"

Footsteps thundered away from the cellar. Juliet stared at the door. For a terrible instant, she looked as if she might open it anyway. Romeo caught her hand before she could reach the slide.

"She said not to."

Juliet's breathing shook. "She's drawing them away."

"Yes."

"She'll get herself killed."

"She knew exactly what she was doing."

That was the worst part. Juliet saw him then, fully, as if realizing for the first time what kind of woman Galina had been before she became indispensable to her. Above them, the running footsteps faded into the house. Romeo grabbed the nearest switch. Nothing happened. The lights did not work. Had the power been cut?

The basement smelled like old stone, damp earth, wine, dust, and expensive things stored for a future no one fully trusted. Emergency lights had kicked on somewhere deeper in the level, not enough to banish shadow, just enough to break it into shapes. Rows of shelves. Stacked crates. A long table with linens folded at one end. A locked iron gate leading farther down into the older cellar vault. Juliet backed into the darkness below, chest rising hard. Her fingers were still wrapped around Romeo's. Neither of them seemed to notice at first. Then she pulled free, pressing two fingers to the cut at her temple. Blood had begun to bead there.

"You're bleeding," Romeo said.

"So are you."

He glanced at his hand. The knife had opened a shallow line across his palm. His ribs hurt when he breathed. The metallic taste of blood in his mouth. Nothing deep. Nothing that mattered yet.

Juliet turned toward the door. "They were speaking Italian."

"Yes."

"That is what people upstairs will remember."

"I know."

"They'll say Montague."

"They were meant to. But they are not Montague."

Her attention sharpened. "You sound sure."

"I know my father's men," Romeo said. "I know how they move, how they curse, how they clear a room when they think no one important is listening. Those men were not Montague."

"That sounds convenient."

"If they were mine, I wouldn't have had to fight one to reach you."

The answer was too plain to sound rehearsed. Juliet looked him over in the broken emergency light. Blood marked his mouth. Coat torn. Breathing hard from having put himself between her and men who, if he was lying, should have been his own.

"And Galina believes in you," she said.

Juliet stared at her hand, where his blood had marked her fingers during the struggle. "So do I."

A distant crash sounded above them. Both of them froze. They waited, but nothing came toward the cellar.

After several breaths, Juliet let out a slow, uneven exhale. "This is absurd."

Romeo almost laughed from the sheer force of it. "That's your word for tonight?"

"It's not the only one I have."

In the dark, without chandeliers and guests and all the machinery of performance around them, he looked harder. Less polished. There was blood at the edge of his mouth, a fresh bruise already deepening at his jaw, and one shoulder of his coat torn where the attacker had caught him. Nothing about him now belonged to a ballroom, which only made it easier to believe what she had already sensed about him: the elegance was real, but it was not the deepest thing in him.

"You were supposed to be gone," she said.

"I was trying."

"Yes," she said. "Obviously."

Juliet glanced toward the door, then back at him. "But I'm inconveniently relieved."

Then Romeo said, with more honesty than self-preservation, "I couldn't leave."

The emergency light caught one side of her face and left the other in shadow. "Because of the attack?"

"Because of you."

Juliet folded her arms, less from cold than from the need to contain something in herself that had started moving too fast. "You don't know me."

"No," he said. "That doesn't seem to be helping."

"This is the part where I should tell you to leave me alone."

"You could," he replied with his voice trailing off in anticipation of rejection, "and you should."

She held his gaze. "I'm not going to."

Juliet turned her face away briefly, pressing two fingers to her temple where the cut had started to bead fresh blood again. Romeo stepped closer on instinct.

"Let me see."

"It's nothing."

"It's bleeding."

"Everything in this house bleeds eventually."

"Juliet," he said.

She lowered her hand. He touched her face gently enough that she felt the offer before the contact. His thumb brushed once beneath the cut, checking its depth. It was nothing serious. She knew that. He knew that. Neither of them moved away.

"What are you doing?" she asked.

"Trying to decide whether you need stitches."

"That's not what I mean."

"No," he said. "I know."

Juliet faced him directly now, all pretense burned off by adrenaline, fear, and the ruinous relief of being seen without performance. "You're a Montague."

"Yes."

"Do you have any idea what that means in this house?"

"I believe so."

Her gaze narrowed. "No. You do not."

"Then tell me."

"It means," she said slowly, "that your name is the kind men in my family say with their mouths closed, like the word itself tastes bad. It means if my father thought I wanted something from your world, he would call it confusion until he found a way to kill it. It means if Tybalt had recognized you sooner, we would not be having this conversation. And it means"—her voice lowered—"that I should hate what it does to me when you look at me."

"What does it do?"

Juliet's mouth nearly curved. It was a pained thing, more surrender than humor. "It makes me think names are flimsy things. And they aren't."

"A name is blood," he said. "A history. An inheritance. I know that."

"Do you?"

"Yes." He took a breath. "And still—if I had met you anywhere else tonight, with any other family attached to you, I would have wanted you just the same."

"That isn't helping."

"It's not meant to."

"You're incorrigible."

"That seems premature. We've barely begun."

Juliet let out a breath that might have been another laugh if it had not trembled at the end. "You are out of your mind."

"Entirely possible."

Outside the cellar door, footsteps crossed the upper corridor, paused, then faded. They waited. When nothing followed, Juliet leaned back against the stone pillar near the linens table and closed her eyes for a second. Her whole body had started to feel the crash after danger—the shaking in the legs, the delayed awareness of bruises, the pulse that had nowhere to go. Romeo saw it and moved closer again, slower this time.

"You can sit down."

She opened her eyes. "If I sit, I may not stand up gracefully."

"I wasn't aware grace was the priority."

"It is always the priority," she said. "Until people start shooting."

He laughed, low and unwilling. He found an unopened crate against the wall and dragged it closer. Juliet hesitated, then sat, smoothing the torn silk over her knees with the automatic instinct of a woman raised never to appear disordered, even in a basement while her father's enemies fought upstairs. Romeo crouched in front of her.

From here he was slightly below her eye line, which made the moment feel strangely like an oath neither of them had yet spoken. He rested his forearms on his knees and looked up at her like he had nowhere else left to be.

"Do you love this life?" he asked.

Juliet did not answer. No one had ever asked her the question honestly. People asked whether she understood it, whether she appreciated it, whether she was prepared to uphold it. Those were different things.

"No," she said at last.

"Then leave."

She regarded him for a long time.

"You say that as if people just open doors for one another."

"I'd open one."

Juliet felt it everywhere.

"You don't know what you're offering."

"No," he said. "But I know I mean it."

Something in her expression opened then, in a way he had not yet seen. She looked younger for it and more real, because beneath the polish he could finally see the loneliness there—old isolation taught by surveillance, family power, and tenderness smuggled in as discipline.

"You really did come back for me," she said.

"Yes."

"Why?"

He could not give her a simple answer for what he felt, because he did not truly understand why this woman meant so much to him. It felt like being pulled toward her, like gravity.

"Because when I left that room," he said, "it felt off to go where you weren't."

Juliet's fingers tightened in the torn silk at her knees. The cellar was quiet except for their breathing and the faint, distant noise of men restoring order somewhere above them. Romeo could feel the whole future of the night pressing on this moment like a weight, one choice becoming the argument for the next. He stood slowly, and Juliet rose too, drawn up by something stronger than caution.

When he kissed her this time, there was no ballroom left in either of them. No music. No guests. No masks. Just the cool cellar air and the heat that surged between them when fear had already stripped every word down to its true value.

The kiss was deeper than the first, slower only at the start. Her hands found his coat and held. His hand went to the back of her neck, then to her waist, careful even in want. He felt the tremor run through her and knew, with a jolt that was part wonder and part ruin, that she was not trembling from fear anymore. When they broke apart, Juliet rested her forehead briefly against his chest.

Neither of them moved. For one fragile measure of time, they simply stood there, taking comfort in each other and in the unlikely warmth of being alive together. Then something caught Romeo's eye in the broken emergency light. He bent and picked it up from the stone floor.

"What is it?" Juliet asked.

Romeo held it between two fingers and lifted it toward the light. A small sapphire flashed once, bright and blue in the red wash of the basement lamps.

"I think it's an earring."

Juliet lifted both hands to her ears by instinct. Her fingers found the left sapphire still fastened there, then the empty place at her right.

"It's mine."

He held it out. "Here."

Juliet looked at the earring in his palm. The sight of it—one small piece of her expensive, arranged evening lying in Romeo Montague's hand—made something soften in her chest. She reached for it, then stopped.

"No," she said.

Romeo's eyes lifted to hers.

"Keep it," Juliet said, pushing his hand gently back toward him. A small smile touched her mouth, fragile but real. "So you remember this night."

Romeo's fingers closed slowly around the sapphire.

"As if I could forget."

Then a voice came through the cellar door.

"Juliet."

Galina. Not loud or panicked. Controlled. Juliet stepped away instantly, every instinct back in place.

"Juliet," Galina called softly. "It's me. I have some of your father's men with me. It's safe now. Please open the door."

Juliet turned to Romeo. So much passed in that look—alarm, urgency, reluctance, want—that it felt almost indecent to witness.

"Hide," she whispered.

Romeo scanned the dimly lit room. He found a deep shadow behind the stacked wine crates near the older iron gate and he began to move.

"No," Juliet said, noticing his intention. "Not there."

She crossed quickly to the linen table, seized the edge of one hanging cloth, and pulled it aside. Behind it was a narrow service recess where old wine racks had been removed and never replaced. Dark enough to hide a man if the light did not linger. Useless if anyone knew to look. Romeo slipped into it. Juliet dropped the linen back into place and crossed to the door. She lifted the iron slide. Galina entered first.

Two Kapulet security men followed with weapons low and flashlights up. Galina's hair had come partly loose, and there was blood on one sleeve that did not look like hers. She had recovered her face by then—the servant's face, the guardian's face, the face that made powerful people forget how much she saw. But Juliet knew better now. So did Romeo.

Galina's eyes took in Juliet's torn gown, the blood at her temple, the bruising at her arm where the attacker had grabbed her, and then—very quickly and very intelligently—the linen-draped recess without turning her head enough to reveal that she had noticed.

"Thank God," Galina said, and crossed herself with furious efficiency. "They said you were unaccounted for."

"I'm fine," Juliet said.

"No one is fine."

One of the security men asked, "Is anyone else down here?"

Juliet held herself perfectly still.

"No," she said. "I locked the door when I heard shouting."

The second guard looked past her into the cellar. "There may still be Montague men inside."

"There were no Montague men," Galina said.

Both guards turned to her.

She turned on them with a coldness that made even armed men remember who had helped raise the daughter of the house. "There were Italian voices. That is not the same thing. The attackers moved like hired men and spoke too loudly for professionals who wanted to remain unnamed. Someone wanted you frightened in a specific direction."

The first guard did not like that. "You know this how?"

Galina's lips tightened. "Because I listened before shooting became everyone else's excuse to stop thinking."

The guard swept the room with a flashlight anyway. The beam moved over the stone floor, the locked iron gate, the rows of bottles, the stacked crates, the long table with folded linens. It touched the hanging cloth.

Galina moved toward Juliet at the same moment, lifting a handkerchief to the cut at her temple and shifting just enough to block the line of sight.

"She is bleeding," Galina snapped. "If you want to search wine racks while Viktor's daughter stands injured in a cellar, do it quickly and then explain your priorities to her father."

That worked better than any plea would have. The light moved on.

"We need to get her upstairs," the first guard said.

"At last," Galina replied. "The first sensible thing I have heard muttered by either of you."

The guards stepped into the hall first. Galina guided Juliet to the threshold, then stopped as if remembering something. "After this, I am going to St. Ignatius," Galina said. "Some of us still pray when men run out of sense."

Chapter 10. Tuesday Late Night — Alley Behind the Kapulet Townhouse, Georgetown

By the time Romeo slipped out through the rear service alley, the house had already begun lying about what had happened inside it. Music had resumed somewhere beyond the brick walls. Not loudly. Not convincingly. Just enough for the street to hear that the evening still considered itself salvageable. Security had tightened at both ends of the block. Staff with pale faces carried broken glass and stained linens through the rear gate as if the only emergency worth mentioning was carelessness with crystal. Romeo kept to the alley wall, one shoulder brushing wet brick, his breath rough in his chest. His hand was stained. Some of it was his. Some of it was not.

He was nearly at the mouth of the alley when Benvolio stepped out of the dark and caught him by the sleeve. Romeo did not even flinch.

"There you are," Benvolio said, low and furious.

Mercutio emerged from deeper shadow, coat collar turned up, face too bright for the situation. "You live. Wonderful. I was beginning to prepare an emotionally sincere speech to your father, and I resent you for nearly forcing that on me."

Romeo pulled free, but his eyes went back to the house. Benvolio saw the look. Not fear or caution. Something worse.

"Don't," Benvolio said.

Romeo kept staring at the dark rear windows. "Don't what?"

"Whatever your face is about to become."

Mercutio stepped closer and noticed the torn shoulder of Romeo's coat. Then the blood. His smile thinned.

"Well," he said. "That is more blood than I prefer on a friend immediately after a party."

Benvolio's anger shifted, sharpened by dread. "Are you shot?"

"No."

"Then whose blood is that?"

Romeo looked down at his hand as if seeing it for the first time.

"One of them."

The alley changed around the words. Mercutio stopped moving.

Benvolio's grip tightened around the coffee-cold rage in his chest. "One of who?"

"The men inside."

"You killed one?"

Romeo nodded once.

Benvolio turned toward the rear gate. "Jesus."

"He had Juliet."

That ended the next question before Benvolio could ask it.

Mercutio's voice came softer than usual. "Had her how?"

"By the wrist. Knife coming out. Galina was fighting him. Juliet kicked his hand. I got the blade first."

Mercutio grabbed Romeo's shoulder. "My God, man. Did you kill him?"

Romeo nodded. "I didn't have a choice. It was either him or me."

Benvolio frowned. "I can't believe what I'm hearing."

Mercutio shook his head. "You heard him. He had no choice. You heard the gunshots. He ran in when everyone else was running out."

"And I am a federal agent," Benvolio exclaimed. "I should be doing something—anything—at this moment besides standing in this alley listening to this."

Mercutio stepped in front of Benvolio. "Listen to yourself. No, listen to the house. They're literally playing music after an attack. I don't hear police cars or ambulances. And why is that?" He paused, his voice settling into something solid. "Tell me, Benvolio. Why is that? We're in the heart of D.C. We saw senators, members of Congress, and billionaires in that ballroom. The elite of D.C. were in there, and they're acting like it didn't happen. There's not a damn thing you can do except maybe take care of your friend—your cousin—who ran into that house with no backup and no badge."

Benvolio looked from Mercutio to Romeo. The anger in his face shifted into something colder. "They're controlling the narrative," he said. "And Romeo may be the only witness outside their control." He nodded once. "You're right."

Benvolio moved over to his cousin. "Romeo, forgive me. Are you all right? What can we do?"

Romeo turned to his cousin and his friend. "I'm fine, but I'm worried about Juliet."

Benvolio stammered, "I thought you said Juliet was okay."

"I think she is. She had a cut across her temple, but she was being rushed back inside. Galina is with her. She is tough. I have never seen a woman fight like her, especially at her age."

"Galina?" Benvolio asked. "The attendant? Juliet's nurse?"

Romeo cocked his head appraisingly. "She's more than a nurse or an attendant. She moved like she'd done it before. She took down two attackers while I barely managed one."

Mercutio whistled at that. "Remind me not to make her mad."

"Tell me about it," Romeo said. "She saved me and Juliet. She put us down in the cellar, then spoke fluent Italian while she acted as a diversion."

"She speaks Italian," Benvolio mused. "They were speaking Italian outside too."

Romeo turned to him.

"You heard?"

"Everyone heard," Benvolio said. "That was the point."

Mercutio glanced toward the house. "A bit theatrical for professionals, wasn't it?"

"Yes," Benvolio said. "Too theatrical."

Romeo wiped his bleeding palm against the side of his trousers without thinking. "They weren't Montague."

"I know."

That got Romeo's full attention.

Benvolio kept his voice low. "If your father's men hit a Kapulet house, they do not shout Italian loud enough for caterers to remember it. They do not leave the language lying around like a calling card."

Mercutio tilted his head. "Unless they've grown suddenly stupid."

"They haven't," Benvolio said.

Romeo stared down the alley, toward the place where the rear door had swung open and men had spilled blood across polished floors. "Juliet said they'll remember the voices."

"They will," Benvolio said. "And whoever sent those men wanted that memory planted before anyone had time to think."

"A false flag," Mercutio said.

Benvolio nodded. "Or close enough to start one."

For a long beat, none of them spoke. The music behind the walls kept playing. A thin, strained waltz, barely audible over the low murmur of radios at the block's end.

Then Romeo said, "I need to see her again."

Benvolio laughed once. It came out badly.

"You have known her for less than one night."

Romeo did not answer.

"She is a Kapulet."

"I know."

"You killed a man in her house."

"I did."

"And somehow none of that is stopping you."

Romeo met his eyes. "No."

Mercutio leaned against the alley wall and regarded Benvolio with a grim little flash of amusement. "I believe reason has formally exited the discussion."

Benvolio rounded on him. "You are not helping."

"I rarely do."

Benvolio faced Romeo. "You are in shock."

"Probably," Romeo shot back. "But this is bigger than just me and Juliet. Someone staged that attack to point at my family. They are trying to start a war. I don't know about you, but talking with Juliet may be the best way to stop that war and find out who is behind this."

Mercutio looked over at Benvolio. "He has a point. This is huge. You told me when you became an FBI agent that you did it to save lives. To save the lives of your family. This is your chance. You step away from this, and you've been living a lie."

Benvolio looked between Mercutio and Romeo in the darkened alley. "You're right. Now how do we make this happen?"

Romeo smiled. "Galina told me right before she left. The key is St. Ignatius. I need to speak to Father Lawrence."

Chapter 11. Wednesday Morning — St. Ignatius Parish, Georgetown

St. Ignatius looked too old to care about Washington. The church sat three blocks from the better restaurants and somehow felt farther from the city than that. Its stone steps dipped in the middle from generations of feet. The brass handles on the front doors had been polished by palms rich, poor, guilty, grieving, and drunk. In the narrow side garden, frost clung to dead ivy and the winter herbs Father Lawrence insisted on keeping alive through stubbornness, prayer, and threats. Romeo found him there.

The priest was bent over a raised bed in a black coat, collar visible above a gray scarf, gardening gloves pulled tight over large, scarred hands. A row of small glass jars sat on the low stone wall beside him. Dried mint. Willow bark. Chamomile. Rosemary. Things he gave to parishioners who trusted old remedies more than hospital bills and rich men who preferred not to explain certain injuries in waiting rooms. Father Lawrence called it parish medicine. Benvolio called it one more reason the old man knew too much.

Without turning, Father Lawrence said, “Too early for confession.”

Romeo stopped at the garden gate.

The priest clipped a dead stem from a rosemary plant and dropped it into a tin pail. “Which means either guilt, trouble, or a woman.”

Romeo said, “What if it’s all three?”

Father Lawrence stilled. Then he turned. He was older than Romeo remembered and somehow less softened by it. Late sixties, maybe. Narrow face. Keen eyes. A mouth that looked like it had forgiven many people without ever mistaking forgiveness for innocence. The years had thinned his hair and deepened the lines around his eyes, but he still carried himself like a man who knew where every exit was and which men near it were armed. His gaze moved over Romeo’s split lip, bruised jaw, torn coat, and bandaged hand.

“Romeo Montague,” Father Lawrence said. “The last time you came to me looking like that, you were thirteen, bleeding from the mouth, and Mercutio Vale had convinced you that a fistfight behind the parish hall counted as moral education.”

Romeo’s mouth almost twitched. “He said I needed practical theology.”

“What does that even mean?” Father Lawrence gave a faint huff. “He was an incorrigible youth.”

His gaze drifted past Romeo for a moment, as if looking back through the years.

"Do not tell me he is somehow involved in your current disheveled state."

"Not directly."

"That is not comforting." Father Lawrence paused. "I have not seen him in years. At least, not in confession. Tell me, or lie to me if charity requires it: has he become an outstanding leader in the community?"

Romeo's mouth almost twitched again. "So, lie to you, then."

Father Lawrence shook his head. "Never mind. That boy had a gift for making sin sound like civic engagement."

A faint smile touched Romeo's mouth.

Father Lawrence pulled off one glove finger by finger and set it beside the jars. "Benvolio called before sunrise."

Romeo's attention sharpened. "What did he say?"

"That if you appeared, I should hear you before I judged you." The priest looked him over again. "He sounded as if he hated both parts."

"He usually does."

"That boy was born with a conscience and then made the poor decision to work for the federal government. Sit."

Romeo glanced toward the bench under the bare crepe myrtle.

"I don't need to sit."

"You do," Father Lawrence said. "But pride often arrives before circulation."

Romeo sat.

Father Lawrence picked up one of the jars, opened it, and sniffed. "Willow bark," he said. "For pain."

"I'm fine."

"No one with blood under his nails is fine." He examined Romeo's hand. "Yours?"

"Some of it."

"Ah."

The priest closed the jar and sat beside him, leaving enough space between them for truth to enter and still feel unwelcome.

"Start with the part Benvolio did not want to say aloud."

Romeo looked down at his hands.

"The Kapulet house was attacked last night."

"I heard the polite version," Father Lawrence said. "A security concern. A disturbance. No one important hurt. That phrase usually means someone important bled on polished flooring."

"It was not Montague."

Father Lawrence did not react quickly. That was one of his habits. He let claims stand long enough to show whether they had weight.

Romeo continued. "The attackers spoke Italian loudly enough for half the house to remember it. They wanted Kapulet thinking Montague before anyone had time to ask why."

"Did you see them?"

"Yes."

"Did they move like Montague men?"

"No."

"Then someone is trying to make your father's house look guilty."

"Yes."

Father Lawrence turned toward the church wall. The morning traffic beyond it moved quietly, ordinary and blind.

"That kind of lie does not stay inside walls," he said. "Not in this city."

"That's why I'm here."

"No," Father Lawrence said. "That is one reason you are here. Not the first."

Romeo did not answer.

The priest's expression sharpened with faint impatience. "Who is she?"

Romeo looked up. Father Lawrence waited.

"Juliet Kapulet."

The words changed the garden. Not dramatically. No gasp. No cross clutched at the chest. Father Lawrence simply stopped moving. His hand, halfway to another jar, stayed in the air a moment too long before lowering to his knee.

"Juliet Kapulet," he said.

"Yes."

"Viktor Kapulet's daughter."

"Yes."

"The same Juliet Kapulet honored at the masquerade your cousin told me you had no sane reason to attend."

Romeo did not answer. Father Lawrence regarded him.

Then he said, quietly, "No."

"She was targeted," Romeo said, pleading his case.

"Of course she was. Girls like that are rarely allowed to be only daughters."

Romeo leaned forward. "She knows it wasn't us."

"That helps less than you think."

"It helps enough."

Father Lawrence's eyes sharpened. "Careful. That sounds like hope talking before judgment has put its shoes on."

Romeo swallowed whatever answer came first. The priest saw him do it and sighed.

"You were always like this as a boy," Father Lawrence said. "Quiet until the thing mattered, then immovable. Your father thought that meant discipline. I thought it meant danger."

"You knew my father better than I did?"

"No. I knew boys better than he did." Father Lawrence reached for another jar and turned it slowly in his hand. "And I knew this city. Washington feeds on young men who believe wanting the right thing makes them safe."

"I'm not asking to be safe."

"That is exactly what frightens me."

Romeo looked away toward the church doors. "I need to get word to her."

"Why?"

"To know she is alive."

"You already know that."

"To know she is safe."

"In that house? She is not," Father Lawrence said it plainly.

Romeo turned back to him. "Then you understand."

"I understand that two houses are close to war. I understand someone is trying to frame Montague in a room full of Kapulet fear. I understand the streets of D.C. will pay for what powerful men decide to call honor." His voice lowered. "And I understand that if Romeo Montague starts chasing Juliet Kapulet through church doors, alleys, and family guards, the war may not need much help beginning."

Romeo held his gaze. "Then help me stop it."

Father Lawrence stayed quiet.

"The attackers went for her," Romeo said. "Not just the house. Her. If I can speak to Juliet, if she can tell me what she saw, what her family is saying, whether anyone inside is pushing the lie—"

"Do not dress this entirely as investigation," Father Lawrence said.

Romeo fell silent.

The priest regarded him, and there was no cruelty in his face. "You want the truth," Father Lawrence said. "You also want the girl."

"Yes."

The word came out simple enough to make Father Lawrence close his eyes. When he opened them, he looked older. "God preserve us from honest boys," he muttered.

"I'm not a boy."

"You are to me."

Romeo almost objected. Then he remembered being ten years old in this same garden, Mercutio daring him to steal figs from the rectory wall while Father Lawrence pretended not to notice until they had eaten three each and learned the fourth was punishment enough. He remembered Benvolio at twelve, solemn already, asking the priest why bad men got funerals too. He remembered Father Lawrence telling him because death is not where men learn mercy; it is where the living prove whether they ever learned it at all. The memories did not comfort him. They made him feel seen.

Father Lawrence stood and crossed to the garden wall. He lifted the rosemary jar, then set it down again without opening it.

"Who sent you here?" he asked.

"Benvolio."

"No," Father Lawrence said. "Who pointed you here first?"

Romeo hesitated.

"Galina."

The word entered the space between them and stayed there. Father Lawrence did not turn around. He stayed silent. The garden seemed to go tense around him. A car moved somewhere beyond the wall. A bell rang once inside the church, dull and low. Father Lawrence's hand rested on the stone beside the jars, the knuckles pale.

Finally, he said, "Galina Mirov?"

"Yes."

"She told you to come to me?"

"She said St. Ignatius before she left. Somehow she knew I knew you."

Father Lawrence turned then, slowly. Whatever had moved across his face was gone by the time Romeo saw him fully. But not quickly enough. Romeo had seen the pause. The pause. The old weight in it. The priest's voice, when it came, was even.

"Galina does not waste directions."

"You know her."

Father Lawrence held his eyes.

"I know many people."

"You didn't answer the question."

"It is the only answer you are getting this morning."

Romeo let that sit.

Father Lawrence came back to the bench and stood over him. "Listen carefully. If Galina sent the road through this church, then she has already judged three things. First, Juliet is in danger. Second, the official story inside that house is not to be trusted. Third, whatever she saw last night made inaction the greater risk."

"That is what I think."

"You think many things right now. Most of them have her face on them."

Romeo lowered his gaze.

Father Lawrence's tone softened by half a degree. "That does not make them false."

Romeo reached into his coat, then stopped. "I could write her a note."

"No."

"I haven't said what it would say."

"If it begins with Juliet and ends with Romeo, it is already evidence."

Romeo's expression tightened.

The priest saw the emotion pass through him and let it. Then he said, "What you need is not a love letter. What you need is a channel."

"Yes."

"And what the city needs is to know who thought framing Montague inside a Kapulet house was clever enough to risk corpses in the street."

Romeo looked up. Father Lawrence nodded once, not in approval, but in acceptance of the hour.

"I will not promise to help you court Juliet Kapulet."

Romeo's face shifted.

"But," Father Lawrence continued, "I will help keep this city from becoming a battlefield if I can. The last thing I want is war in the streets of D.C. Not between fathers. Not between sons. Not because some third hand wanted both houses blind with rage."

Romeo stood. "Then what do we do?"

"You do nothing."

"Father—"

"You do nothing visible," Father Lawrence corrected. "You go home. You wash. You sleep if your conscience permits it. You do not call her. You do not send a driver. You do not make Benvolio regret having faith in me instead of handcuffs."

Romeo breathed out hard.

Father Lawrence stepped closer. "And remember this: love does not bless every dangerous thing you do in its name. Reckless is still reckless."

Romeo held his gaze.

The priest went on. "If Galina visits, I will speak with her. I will ask what she saw, what Juliet knows, and what lie the Kapulet house is choosing to live inside. Then I will get to the heart of the matter."

Romeo glanced toward the church doors, then back at him. "And Juliet?"

Father Lawrence's face did not soften, but his voice did.

"If there is a safe word to send, Galina will know how to carry it."

"That isn't enough."

"No," Father Lawrence said. "It is what we have."

A bell sounded again inside the church. Father Lawrence picked up his gloves from the wall and pulled one on, then the other.

"Go," he said.

Romeo stayed where he was.

"Romeo."

He looked up.

"If someone is trying to frame the Montague house, they are counting on men to act quickly and badly." Father Lawrence fixed him with a sharper look. "Do not be useful to your enemy."

Slowly, reluctantly, Romeo nodded and turned to walk away. At the garden gate, he paused and glanced behind him. Father Lawrence had already returned to the herb bed, pruning dead stems from a plant that had no business surviving winter and somehow had.

"Father."

The priest did not turn. "Yes?"

"Will Galina come?"

Father Lawrence's shears stilled for one brief second. Then they closed around another dead stem. "She will," he said. "When she is ready."

Romeo left through the side gate. Father Lawrence waited until the latch clicked shut behind him, and only then did he look toward the church.

"Galina," he said under his breath, the word sounding less like surprise than memory. Then he set the shears down, crossed himself once, and went inside to wait.

Chapter 12. Wednesday Late Morning — Confessional, St. Ignatius Parish, Georgetown

Father Lawrence knew Galina had entered the church before he saw her. Some people made noise by accident. Galina Mirov made quiet by choice. She came through the side door just before eleven, dressed in a charcoal coat and dark gloves, a black scarf tied low at her throat. She crossed herself with the quick precision of a woman who had learned long ago that faith and habit sometimes wore the same face. Then she moved down the side aisle without looking left or right. Two Kapulet security men waited outside near the curb.

Father Lawrence had noticed them from the sacristy window ten minutes earlier. One by the black sedan. One under the bare sycamore, pretending to study his phone while his eyes checked every door. They had not come inside. That told Lawrence two things. First, Kapulet security had tightened exactly as expected. Second, Galina still had enough authority to tell armed men where not to stand. That mattered. Galina paused at the candle stand near the Virgin and lit one flame. Only one. Then she turned toward the old confessional. Father Lawrence was already inside.

The confessional sat in the dim north transept, old wood darkened by age and too many whispered sins. The brass latch had lost its shine. The red velvet kneeler inside the penitent's side had worn thin at the center. A narrow screen separated priest from parishioner, though Lawrence had learned over the years that screens rarely hid the truth. They only made people brave enough to say it. Galina opened the door and stepped in. Neither of them spoke.

The faint scent of wax and cold stone rested between them. Somewhere in the nave, an elderly woman coughed once, then returned to prayer. Rain ticked softly against the stained glass.

Father Lawrence said, "Is this confession?"

Galina sat behind the screen. "No."

"Good," he said. "Then I may still lie, interrupt, and give advice you will ignore."

A small pause followed.

Then Galina said, "You have not changed as much as you think."

His hand, resting on the worn arm of the chair, stilled.

"Neither have you," he said.

"That is not a compliment."

"It was not meant as one."

The faintest breath left her. Almost a laugh. Almost not.

Father Lawrence turned slightly, though the screen kept her face broken into shadow and shape. "How are you?"

Galina did not answer quickly. That, more than anything, told him the truth.

"At my age," she said at last, "one becomes careful with questions like that."

"At your age," he said, "you have earned the right to answer badly."

"I am alive. Bruised. Angry. Tired of men with weapons mistaking noise for courage."

"Then you are yourself."

Her mouth shifted in the dimness. "And you?"

"Old," he said. "Irritated. In possession of more herbs than sense."

"That was always true."

Outside the confessional, the church went tense around them.

Father Lawrence lowered his voice. "Tell me what happened."

"You have Romeo's version."

"Yes," Father Lawrence said, "but his version is too emotional. He does not have a trained eye like you do."

She looked down at the tin in her palm, then tucked it into her coat pocket. "The attackers came through the rear service line. Not drunk men. Not street trash. Trained. Fast. They knew where to push. They knew the house would turn inward before anyone outside understood what was happening."

"They wanted Juliet?"

"Yes."

The answer came too plainly for comfort. Father Lawrence closed his eyes once.

Galina continued, "They spoke Italian loudly enough for servants to remember it. Loudly enough for men who do not understand Italian to repeat the word Montague with confidence."

"Not Montague, then."

"No."

"You are sure?"

"I am old, not foolish."

Father Lawrence chuckled. "No. Foolish has never been one of your sins."

Her voice hardened. "Romeo fought them."

Father Lawrence waited.

"One of them had Juliet by the wrist," Galina said. "A blade coming out. I was occupied with another. Juliet kicked his hand. Romeo got the knife first."

"And killed him."

"Yes."

The church seemed colder around the word.

Galina did not soften it. "He saved her. She helped save him. And that"—she paused—"makes everything more complicated."

Father Lawrence let the word sit. Complicated. It was the kind of word people reached for when the truth had become too alive to stay orderly. Romeo had sat with him that morning wearing bruises, blood, and the stubborn fear of a man more worried for a Kapulet girl than for his own safety. That sort of feeling could be grace, if guided. It could also become a match dropped into dry streets.

Emotion had its place. Father Lawrence had spent his life learning that. It moved people toward mercy, courage, even sacrifice. But in houses like Montague and Kapulet, emotion rarely stayed clean for long. Love became loyalty. Loyalty became revenge. Revenge became bodies in alleys while older men called it honor. And yet Galina had seen something. He heard it in what she did not say quickly.

"That impressed you."

"It reassured me." A pause. "Impressed is too generous."

"Galina."

She sighed. "Yes. He is everything you said he was, and the act impressed me. Not so much the technique. That was sloppy."

A faint smile touched Father Lawrence's mouth. Almost.

"And Juliet?" he asked.

Galina's quiet changed. It was slight, but he knew her silences. Some were shields. Some were knives. This one was pain standing upright.

"Juliet is not merely grateful," she said.

"No."

"She asks after Romeo before she asks after herself. When Paris's flowers came, she regarded them as if they had been sent by a polite disease."

Father Lawrence's expression tightened. "Paris has moved already?"

Galina frowned, a silent yes passing over her expression. "I witnessed a heated exchange between Paris and Ekaterina following the attack, before they shut the library door. Not an hour later, flowers and a card arrived. Concern arranged in flawless handwriting on a card." Galina's voice cooled. "Ekaterina approves of him even more after the attack and advocates for him."

"And Viktor?"

"He listens to Ekaterina, but he is quiet, brooding in his thoughts."

"That is worse."

"Yes."

Galina shifted on the kneeler. The old wood gave a faint complaint beneath her. "Security is tight. Two men at the front. Two at the garden. One near the east stairs. The rear service passage is sealed. Staff are being counted like spoons. Tybalt is in charge, and he is quite efficient. This is his niche in life."

"Does he know?"

"About Romeo and Juliet? Not about the cellar, only about the dance. With Tybalt, that is more than enough."

Father Lawrence rubbed one hand over his mouth. This city, he thought, never lacked men willing to turn suspicion into violence.

Galina said, "They will blame Montague if given time."

"They are already being given time."

"Yes."

"And Salvatore will not accept blame quietly."

"No."

"Then someone is pushing both houses toward the street."

"Yes."

The word passed through the screen and settled between them. War. Neither said it at first. They did not have to.

Father Lawrence glanced toward the narrow strip of light beneath the confessional door. "If Kapulet moves in anger and Montague answers in pride, this city pays before either father admits he was used."

"Washington will call it organized crime," Galina said. "The dead will call it Thursday."

He turned toward the screen. Her voice had not changed, but the old wound in it was unmistakable.

"You think I am exaggerating?" she asked.

"No," he said. "I think you are understating it because you dislike melodrama."

"I dislike incompetence. Melodrama is only incompetence with better clothes."

This time he did smile. Briefly, through the screen, she did too. Then the smile faded.

"They are so similar," Galina said.

"Romeo and Juliet?"

"Yes." She drew in a slow breath. "Different houses. Same cage. Both raised under names too heavy for them. Both watched by people who call it love when they mean control. Both lonely enough to recognize the other too quickly."

Father Lawrence was quiet.

Galina's voice softened despite herself. "I saw them in the cellar. Not long. Not enough for foolish certainty, perhaps. But enough to know something had already happened."

"Something happened," Father Lawrence said. "Words mean things, Galina. Be careful what you call."

"Words do mean things," she said. "Daughter. Son. Honor. We speak them every day as if they are blessings, then act surprised when they demand violence."

He lowered his eyes. There were moments when she sounded exactly as she had years ago, before age and discipline and all the roles they had survived wearing. The same clarity. The same refusal to decorate fear.

He said, "You do not want to hold Juliet back."

"I want to lock her in her room and stand outside it with a gun until every man in this city dies of old age."

"That is one option."

"It lacks elegance."

"It has simplicity."

"She would hate me," Galina said.

"She might live."

"She would live smaller."

Father Lawrence felt the shift in her behind the screen.

"I will not help them bury her in silk," she said. "Not if there is another road."

"And Romeo is that road?"

"No." Her answer came quickly. "Romeo is a boy with blood on his hands and love moving faster than judgment. He is not a road. He is a risk."

"Then why are you here?"

"Because doing nothing is also a risk."

Father Lawrence bowed his head once. Yes. There it was. The truth both of them had known before she crossed the nave.

Galina said, "You told him to wait for me."

"I told him to do nothing visible."

"Did he listen?"

"For now."

"That sounds temporary."

"He is twenty-something, wounded, and in love with a Kapulet. Temporary is the best virtue available."

Galina let out a low breath. "God help us."

"He has been asked."

"And did He answer?"

"In my experience, He often waits until the worst possible moment and then gives instructions no sane person would call practical."

"Then He must enjoy Washington."

Father Lawrence gave a tired smile, then let it go.

"We need a channel," he said.

"Yes."

"No letters through drivers. No phones. No staff unless you trust them with your life."

"I trust very few people with my life."

"I remember."

The words came out before he could stop them. A pause followed. Not empty quiet. Not awkward. Something older. Something that knew exactly where not to step.

Galina's voice, when it came, was quieter. "Do you?"

"Yes."

The church around them seemed to recede. For a brief span, there was no Kapulet, no Montague, no Romeo, no Juliet. Only two people divided by a wooden screen, speaking through a space that had once held sins easier to confess than regret. Galina broke the moment first.

"What do you propose?"

Father Lawrence let the question steady him.

"Juliet comes here."

"Impossible."

"No. Difficult."

"She is watched."

"She was attacked. She is frightened. No mother in this city who cares about appearances will forbid confession if the request is made properly."

"Ekaterina is not most mothers."

"No," he said. "But she understands optics better than most. A shaken daughter seeking a priest after violence looks orderly. Manageable. Pious, even."

Galina considered. He could feel her doing it: measuring doors, guards, habits, maternal vanity, Viktor's quiet, Tybalt's suspicion, the distance from townhouse to church.

"Juliet could ask," Galina said. "If I make it sound like recovery instead of rebellion."

"Good."

"And Romeo?"

"I will ensure Romeo comes to confession."

Galina's mouth almost curved. "He has sins enough."

"He has more intention than sin at the moment. That worries me more."

"How will you keep them private?"

"The east confessional," he said. "The old double booth near the lower chapel entrance. It has two penitent stalls and a center screen. From the nave, it looks ordinary. I will sit long enough for any watcher to see my cassock through the grille. Then I step out through the inner side door and stand guard."

"You would leave them alone in a confessional?"

"Briefly."

"That is either clever or sacrilegious."

"I have made my peace with being both when necessary."

Galina was silent for another moment.

Then she said, "How long?"

"Ten minutes."

"That is nothing."

"It is more than they have."

"What do they say to each other in ten minutes?"

"The truth, if they have any sense."

"They are in love. Sense will have to be supplied by others."

Father Lawrence laughed. It was small. Brief. So unexpected that the sound seemed to startle both of them.

Then she said, "She will want to see him."

"Yes."

"He will want to see her."

"Yes."

"And we are fools for allowing it."

"Yes."

"But if we do not, they will find another way."

"A worse one."

"Almost certainly."

Father Lawrence glanced toward the thin light under the door again. "Then we give them the least foolish path and pray they do not make it worse."

"Prayer again."

"It is a church."

"So you keep reminding me."

A footstep sounded in the nave. Both of them stilled. The step passed. A woman's low murmur followed, then the faint creak of a pew. Galina exhaled soundlessly.

Father Lawrence leaned closer to the screen. "When?"

"This afternoon, perhaps. Tomorrow if Ekaterina becomes difficult."

"Today is better."

"I know."

"After lunch. Shock wears people down after lunch."

"You always did understand households."

"I understand tyrants. Households are only tyrannies with linens."

"Careful, Lawrence," Galina said.

His hand tightened once on the armrest.

"Yes."

"If this begins a war—"

"It has already begun."

"No," she said. "Not fully. Not yet. There is still a difference between men circling with knives and men sending boys into the streets."

Father Lawrence lowered his eyes. She was right. That was the cruelty of it. They had not yet reached the worst thing. There was still time to prevent it—or cause it faster.

"The last thing I want is war in D.C.," he said.

"Want has nothing to do with it."

"No," he said. "But choice does."

"Choice," Galina said, almost bitterly. "The young keep believing in it."

"And the old keep stealing it from them, then calling the theft wisdom."

Another pause. At last Galina opened the confessional door. Light from the nave cut around her figure. She stepped out but did not immediately leave. Father Lawrence remained seated on his side, separated from her now only by old wood and all the things neither of them had said.

"I will bring Juliet if I can," she said.

"I will bring Romeo."

Galina adjusted her gloves. For the first time since entering the church, the severity in her face softened into something unmistakably fond.

"Be careful, Lawrence."

He stood inside the confessional, one hand on the narrow door.

"You first, Galina."

She looked back once. Briefly, the years between them thinned. Then she turned and walked down the side aisle toward the waiting men, the candle she had lit still burning behind her. Father Lawrence watched until the side door closed and the church settled again into wax, stone, and the quiet before whatever came next.

Chapter 13. Wednesday Late Morning — Coffeehouse Near St. Ignatius Parish, Georgetown

The coffeehouse was narrow, crowded, and warm enough to make everyone inside believe the city outside had become someone else's problem. Benvolio knew better. He sat at a small table near the back wall, where he could see the front door, the side exit, and the reflection of the street in the darkened espresso machine behind the counter. Habit had chosen the seat before thought had finished arriving. His coat remained buttoned. His coffee sat untouched. His phone lay facedown beside his hand.

Mercutio sat opposite him with a pastry he had no intention of finishing and the calm, faintly amused expression of a man who regarded danger as a social inconvenience until it proved otherwise.

"You keep looking at the door," Mercutio said.

"I like doors."

"You like exits. Doors are merely the optimistic version."

Benvolio did not smile.

Mercutio tore off a corner of the pastry and considered it. "That bad?"

"Yes."

"Excellent. I see that your mood is more dour than normal. That is remarkable; I did not think it was possible."

Benvolio turned his phone over and slid it across the table. Mercutio glanced down. A photograph of a cream envelope filled the screen. Thick paper. No return address. Delivered by hand to the Montague house less than an hour ago.

Mercutio's mouth curved. "Tybalt has stationery. Somehow that makes him worse."

"Read."

Mercutio enlarged the image and scanned the message. The note was short. Too short. Salvatore Montague: Your son was seen in my uncle's house on the night blood was spilled. I ask whether he returned home safely. Tybalt Kapulet

Mercutio looked up. "That is beautifully unpleasant."

"It is a threat," Benvolio repeated.

Mercutio sat back, all mockery thinning into attention. "Delivered to Salvatore, not Romeo."

"Yes."

"So he is not merely angry at Romeo. He wants the Montague house to know he knows."

"Or he wants Salvatore to react before anyone thinks clearly."

Mercutio glanced at the note again. "Tybalt always did enjoy making violence feel grammatical."

Benvolio took the phone back. "This is not a duel invitation from some bored aristocrat."

"No. Tybalt lacks the romantic discipline for duels."

"Mercutio."

"What? I am agreeing with you."

"You are insulting him."

"I can do both."

Benvolio finally picked up his coffee, more to have something in his hand than because he wanted it. "Escalus is involved."

That made Mercutio's face sharpen. "Is he?"

"Before dawn. The Kapulet house contained the breach publicly, but not completely. Too many people were there. Too many private security teams. Too many federal interests in one ballroom pretending not to hear gunfire. Escalus has people asking questions, quietly for now."

"Quietly never lasts."

"No."

Mercutio turned toward the window. Outside, Georgetown moved in its usual polished rhythm: dark coats, black umbrellas, delivery vans, students with headphones, and a lobbyist laughing too loudly into a phone. The city had perfected the art of pretending everything was normal, even when it was not.

Mercutio said, "How close are we?"

"To what?"

"To the thing everyone keeps pretending isn't war."

Benvolio's mouth tightened. "Closer than yesterday."

Mercutio paused, then turned to face him. "Kapulet thinks Montague staged the attack?"

"Some in that house want to believe it. Some know better. Some do not care as long as the belief is useful."

"And Montague?"

"Salvatore is quiet."

Mercutio gave a soft, humorless laugh. "That is much worse than shouting."

"Yes."

"And Romeo?"

Benvolio glanced toward the door again.

Mercutio noticed. "Ah."

"He went to Father Lawrence."

"As planned?"

"As planned," Benvolio said, though the word planned felt too generous for what they were doing. "If the priest has any sense, he would turn him away."

"If Father Lawrence had sense, he would have chosen a parish in a boring city."

Benvolio gave him a look.

Mercutio lifted both hands. "I respect the man. I merely question his appetite for doomed youth."

"Romeo is not doomed."

Mercutio's expression softened in a way he would have denied if named. "No. Of course not."

Benvolio hated him a little for that tone.

"He is in shock," Benvolio said. "He killed a man last night. He saved Juliet Kapulet. He thinks that means something."

"It does mean something."

"Tybalt doesn't know, and I don't think he would care. Tybalt knows Romeo was at the party, the same party at which they were attacked. That makes Romeo the natural target for Tybalt."

Mercutio's eyes dropped briefly to the phone. "Tybalt was always going to come looking. If it wasn't last night at the party, it would be something else. That man seeks violence the way a moth seeks a flame."

"Yes, but now he has a reason he can make sound noble."

"Honor," Mercutio said with distaste. "The word men use when vanity wants a knife."

Benvolio leaned forward. "Do not underestimate him."

"I don't underestimate him. I dislike him. That is not the same thing."

"You talk as if he is some overbred knife collector with impulse control problems."

"Is he not?"

"No." Benvolio's voice lowered. "He is trained, connected, and patient when patience suits him. Nothing ever sticks to him long enough for court. That is the problem. A burned warehouse in Norfolk. A witness in Alexandria who recanted after his son disappeared for six hours. Two dock contractors who changed statements after meeting with Kapulet security. A courier found dead in a parking garage with no usable footage anywhere around him. Tybalt never appears where it can be used. His shadow only appears near things."

Mercutio had gone still.

Benvolio continued. "I have seen files with his shadow all over them and nothing a prosecutor could take before a judge without getting laughed out of the room. He knows exactly how much distance the law requires, and he keeps one elegant step behind it."

Mercutio's face hardened. "Yet he pulled a knife on you."

"On the courthouse steps," Benvolio said. "In daylight. In front of deputies, reporters, cameras, and Escalus himself. That is what worries me."

"Because he was careless?"

"No. Because he was not afraid."

The coffeehouse noise seemed to thin around that. A milk steamer hissed. Cups clinked. Someone near the window laughed at something on a laptop. Ordinary life continued, stupid and breakable.

Mercutio turned toward the street. "Tybalt flashes a knife at a federal agent, gets checked by Escalus, then sends a polite death note to the Montague house after Romeo is seen near Juliet. That is not a man cooling down."

"No."

"That is a man choosing a stage."

"Yes."

Mercutio tapped one finger against the table. "And Romeo is walking toward the center of it with flowers in his eyes."

Benvolio did not answer.

Mercutio's attention snapped to him. "That was not a joke."

"I know."

For a long second, both men sat in the warm little coffeehouse and listened to Washington pretending nothing had begun.

Then Mercutio said, more quietly, "He looked different last night."

Benvolio's eyes lifted.

"Romeo," Mercutio said. "In the alley. I have seen him wounded. Angry. Grieving. Bored enough to become reckless. This was not that."

"No."

"He has decided something."

"He barely knows her."

Mercutio gave him a sad, quick smile. "That has never stopped anyone interesting."

"It should stop him."

"It won't."

Benvolio stared at his cold coffee. "I know."

The admission cost him more than he expected.

Mercutio leaned back. "Then our task is not to stop the love. How dreary. It is to keep the love from becoming evidence, motive, or corpse."

"That may be the least romantic sentence you have ever said."

"Romance survives better when someone unromantic handles logistics."

Benvolio nearly smiled despite himself. Almost. His phone buzzed once. Both men turned to it. Benvolio checked the message, read it twice, then placed the phone facedown again. Mercutio waited.

"Escalus wants me available this afternoon," Benvolio said. "Unofficially."

"That means officially soon."

"Yes."

"And Romeo?"

"Needs to stay out of sight."

Mercutio laughed once under his breath. "Romeo Montague. Newly in love. Being asked to stay out of sight. Wonderful."

Benvolio stood, taking his coat from the back of the chair. "Find him if Father Lawrence lets him leave before I do."

Mercutio rose too. "And say what?"

Benvolio glanced toward the front window, where a black SUV rolled slowly past before continuing down the block.

"Tell him Tybalt is asking after him."

Mercutio's face lost the last of its humor.

"That all?"

"No," Benvolio said. "Tell him asking is not the perilous part."

Mercutio nodded once. Outside, the bells of St. Ignatius began to ring noon over Georgetown. Neither man moved until the last bell faded. Then they left the coffeehouse separately, carrying the same knowledge into the cold. Washington was not at war yet. But it had started choosing sides.

Chapter 14. Wednesday Afternoon — East Confessional, St. Ignatius Parish, Georgetown

The Kapulet guards did not like church. Juliet could tell by the way they stood outside the nave, too stiff for prayer and too watchful for reverence. One remained near the side entrance with his coat buttoned and his eyes on the street. The other had followed her and Galina inside, stopping only when Father Lawrence appeared at the end of the aisle and gave him the kind of look old priests reserved for men who had forgotten which ground they were standing on.

"Confession is private," Father Lawrence said.

The guard hesitated. "I have orders."

"So do I," Father Lawrence said flatly. He lifted one finger toward the sky. "Mine come from a higher power."

The guard looked past him toward Galina.

Galina removed one glove finger by finger. "Mrs. Kapulet wanted her daughter seen at prayer, not heard at it."

That settled it. Not because the man liked the answer. Because he understood the authority behind it. He retreated to the rear of the church, where he could see the side door and most of the nave but not the old east confessional near the lower chapel stairs. Father Lawrence watched him go. Then he turned to Juliet.

"You look tired."

"I keep hearing that."

"Then we are beginning honestly."

Juliet did not smile. The church was colder than she remembered. Morning rain had darkened the stone steps outside, and the damp seemed to have followed them in, clinging to the old wood, the candle smoke, the worn kneelers, the saints looking down with painted patience. Somewhere near the front, an elderly woman prayed with a rosary moving steadily through her fingers. Two candles burned near the Virgin. One of them was Galina's. Galina stood at her shoulder, severe and quiet.

Father Lawrence glanced once toward the rear guard, then toward the confessional. "Come."

The east confessional was older than the rest of the church seemed willing to admit. Dark wood, narrow doors, brass latches rubbed dull by generations of hands. It was a double booth, built with a priest's center compartment between two small penitent stalls. From the nave, it looked ordinary. From close up, Juliet saw what Father Lawrence had chosen carefully: too many panels, too many shadows, too many small doors for a modern architect to tolerate. Galina noticed too.

"Convenient," she murmured.

Father Lawrence regarded her. "Historic."

"Of course."

Juliet looked between them. Their faces gave away nothing. That was how she knew both of them were lying. Father Lawrence opened the left penitent door for Juliet. Juliet entered the stall.

It was narrow enough that her shoulder brushed the wall when she lowered herself to the kneeler. The wood smelled faintly of polish, dust, and old breath. A carved screen separated her from the priest's compartment, the small sliding panel already open. Through it, she could see the dark sleeve of Father Lawrence's cassock as he sat. On the other side of him, beyond another screen, there was only shadow. Her pulse changed.

Father Lawrence said, louder than necessary, "Begin when ready."

The guard at the back of the church could hear tone, not words. Juliet bowed her head.

The formal words had never felt more absurd. Still, she whispered, "Bless me, Father, for I have sinned."

She paused as a fresh sound came from the other side of the center compartment. Not from Father Lawrence. Juliet stilled. Father Lawrence slid the panel shut between them. The confessional became dark. Then she heard the soft scrape of the priest rising. His cassock shifted. A latch clicked somewhere inside the center booth. His voice lowered to a thread.

"Ten minutes. If either of you wastes them, I will be deeply annoyed."

The inner door closed. A second passed. Then the panel on Juliet's side opened again. Romeo was there. Not in the opposite stall now. In the priest's narrow center compartment, one hand braced against the carved wood, his face half in shadow. The bruise along his jaw had darkened since last night. The cut at his mouth was healing badly. A bandage wrapped his right hand. He looked as if he had not slept, and as if sleep would have done nothing helpful even if he had tried. Neither of them spoke. Everything she had planned to say vanished.

Romeo watched her as if the sight of her standing, breathing, whole enough to be furious, had struck him deeper than the attack.

"Juliet."

Hearing him say it nearly undid her. She reached through the open panel before caution could stop her. His hand met hers at once, fingers closing around hers through the narrow space.

"You're hurt," she said.

"So are you."

"This is not a competition."

"If it were, you'd win. Your bandage is more graceful."

A laugh broke out of her before she could stop it. Too soft, almost soundless, but real enough to make his face change.

"I'm serious," she whispered.

"So am I."

His thumb moved over her knuckles. The contact was small. Barely anything. And yet she felt it through her whole body.

"You came," he said.

"You sent for me."

"I asked if you were safe."

"I'm not."

His fingers tightened.

Juliet held his gaze. "But I'm here."

Something in him absorbed that and did not know where to put it. They were still holding hands. Neither let go.

Romeo checked her temple. "Does it hurt?"

"It did. Less now."

"Did they call a doctor?"

"House doctor. Quietly. No hospital. No police. No outside record. The house is very committed to pretending glass is the only thing that broke."

His jaw set. "They're building the lie."

"They already have." Juliet looked down at their joined hands. "Security says Montague. Tybalt says Montague. Some of the staff repeat Italian as if language itself is proof."

"The attackers were not ours."

"I know."

He saw her then, fully.

"I know," she said again. "I saw you fight them. I saw you bleed for me."

"That doesn't prove everything."

"No," Juliet said. "But it proves enough."

For one suspended instant, the church disappeared. Not the stone, not the scent of wax, not the terrible fact that they were speaking through a confessional screen while armed men waited outside. Those things remained. But they became less important than the look passing between them: recognition, fear, relief, and the unbearable knowledge that both of them had already chosen more than prudence allowed.

Romeo's voice lowered. "Tybalt sent a letter to my father."

Juliet's chest tightened. "What kind of letter?"

"The polite kind that means violence if you read it correctly. He asked whether I returned home safely."

Juliet shut her eyes once. Of course Tybalt had. A direct threat would have been too crude for the mood he was in. Tybalt liked language when it sharpened the blade before the hand moved.

"He's a threat," Juliet said.

"I know."

"No," Juliet said, and the force in her own voice surprised her. "You do not know. Tybalt does not forget humiliation. My father stopped him in front of everyone. Then the house was attacked. Then you vanished. If he suspects I helped you—"

"He won't get near you."

The words came too fast. Juliet faced him. Romeo realized what he had said and hated, instantly, how little power stood behind it.

"I'm sorry," he said.

"For wanting to protect me?"

"For saying it like wanting was enough."

She drew his hand closer through the screen. "In my house, men often confuse wanting control with wanting safety. You didn't."

"I might, if I'm afraid enough."

"No," she said. "You stopped yourself."

That mattered more than it should have.

Romeo looked down at their hands. "Benvolio says the city is closer to war than yesterday."

"Galina says the same."

"Escalus is already involved."

"I know. My father hates that."

"Mine will too."

Juliet gave him a faint, bitter smile. "Then perhaps the two houses have finally found common ground."

Juliet paused and then said, "Paris came this morning."

Romeo's expression sharpened. Juliet saw it and nearly smiled, though there was nothing amusing about Paris Sokol.

"Flowers first," she said. "Then concern. Then a visit arranged by my mother as if he had been summoned from a shelf labeled safe and security."

Romeo's jaw flexed. "Did he touch you?"

"No."

The answer was immediate.

Then, because she saw what the question had cost him, she added, "He did not need to. That is what makes him a threat."

Romeo's eyes lifted.

Juliet continued, voice low. "Paris does not push like a brute. He waits where my parents want him. He says reasonable things in reasonable rooms. He makes obedience sound mature. He makes escape sound childish. My mother looks at him and sees a locked door with manners."

"And you?"

"I see the lock."

Romeo breathed out through his nose. The anger in him was quiet but visible. It did not make him loud. It made him very still.

"Does he know about me?"

"Not enough."

"That will change."

"Yes."

The word sat there.

Juliet's thumb moved once across his bandaged palm. "What did Benvolio say?"

"That I should stop."

"He sounds intelligent."

"He is."

"And you ignored him?"

"I came here, didn't I?"

"That sounds less intelligent."

"It is."

Juliet looked up. "Then why?"

His eyes held hers through the carved opening.

"Because I woke this morning and the world had become very simple. Not safe. Not easy. Just simple." His voice roughened. "I needed to know whether you were alive. Then I needed to know whether you wanted me gone.

Everything else—my father, your father, Tybalt, Paris, the lie they're building—it all mattered, but none of it came first."

She wanted to answer lightly. She could not.

"What came first?"

"You."

The word moved through the confessional like a thing not meant to be spoken there. Juliet faltered, and Romeo did not dress it up. Did not smile. Did not make it charming or safer than it was. He simply watched her with the terrible sincerity that had undone her first in the ballroom, then in the cellar, and now here, beneath carved saints and old wood.

"You can't say things like that in a confessional," she whispered.

His mouth almost moved. "Isn't this where truth is meant to happen?"

"Not that kind."

"No?"

"No," she said, though her hand tightened around his.

Outside, Galina's voice cut softly through the church air. Calm. Stern. Buying time.

Romeo turned toward the sound, then back to Juliet. "If you tell me to stay away, I will."

Juliet stilled.

He went on, each word careful now. "Not because I want to. Not because it would be easy. But because you have enough people deciding your life for you. I won't become another."

Her throat tightened.

"That is unfair," she said.

"It was meant to be the opposite."

"It is unfair because now I have to answer honestly."

He waited. Juliet looked down at their hands. His fingers were warm despite the cold church. There was blood under one nail he had not managed to wash away. She should have recoiled from it. Instead, she thought of the cellar, of the blade coming free, of Romeo moving before common sense had time to save him from bravery.

"I should tell you to stay away," she said.

"I know."

"I should say I am grateful you saved me, and sorry for what this has become, and wise enough to end it here."

His expression shifted only slightly.

"And are you?" he asked.

"Wise?"

"Yes."

"No."

He released a breath he had been holding.

Juliet leaned closer to the screen. "I don't want you gone."

Romeo's hand shifted on hers, tightening once.

"I don't know what this is," she said. "Not fully. It is too fast. Too reckless. Too full of blood already. But I know what it is not."

"What?"

"It is not only shock."

His eyes closed briefly. When he opened them, the look in them had changed. Softer, yes. But also hungrier. Juliet saw it and felt heat rise low in her body, startling and bright. The confessional suddenly felt smaller, and the screen between them felt like an insult. Romeo's thumb brushed the inside of her wrist, where her pulse had become too obvious to hide.

"Juliet."

"Don't say it like that."

"How am I saying it?"

"Like you already know where my courage ends."

His gaze dropped to her mouth.

"I don't," he said. "But I'm beginning to want to find out."

The words should have offended her. They did not. They lit through her instead, reckless and bright. Juliet looked once toward the confessional door, toward the nave, toward the guard in the rear and Galina somewhere beyond him, holding the world at bay by force of will. Then she looked back at Romeo.

"This is sacrilegious."

"Yes."

"Possibly foolish."

"Definitely."

"And if Father Lawrence comes back—"

"He'll disapprove."

"He already does."

That almost made Romeo smile. Juliet moved first. She slipped the latch on her side of the penitent stall and stepped into the priest's narrow center compartment. Romeo caught her as she entered because there was almost no room between the little chair, the wood walls, and his body. They stood too close to pretend anything. Her skirt brushed his legs. His bandaged hand settled at her waist, careful and not careful enough. The dark wood pressed at her back. The confessional held them like a secret.

"You should not have opened the door," Romeo said.

"You should not have been waiting behind it."

"I was told to confess."

Juliet's mouth curved. "Then confess."

His eyes moved over her face.

"I want you."

The words were low and rough and did something wicked to the air between them.

Juliet lifted her chin. "That was direct."

"I'm trying not to lie in church."

"Then say the rest."

His hand tightened at her waist, not pulling yet, only admitting what restraint was costing him.

"I want to kiss you until I forget where we are," he said. "I want to touch you in ways that would make this booth burst into flames if God were paying close attention."

Juliet faltered. The church did not burst into flames. That seemed, to Juliet, very close to permission. She caught the front of his coat and pulled him down. The kiss was not gentle.

It had been gentle in the ballroom because loss had softened it. Desperate in the cellar because fear had forced truth into their mouths. This was different. This was choice. Narrow, stolen, dangerous choice in a place built for repentance, and neither of them was sorry enough to stop.

Romeo's mouth opened under hers. His hand slid to the small of her back, low enough to make her inhale against him, high enough to prove he was still fighting for control. Juliet's fingers went into his hair. He made a sound against her mouth, rough and quiet, and the sound thrilled her more than it should have. She pressed closer.

There was barely room to move. That made everything worse. Better. His thigh shifted between the folds of her skirt. Her back hit the carved wall. The old wood gave a faint complaint beneath her shoulder blades.

Romeo drew back just enough to breathe. "Juliet."

"If you ask whether I'm sure, I'll be offended."

"I was going to ask whether the door locks."

She stared at him. Then a laugh escaped her, breathless and shocked. Romeo smiled against her mouth, and that small ordinary flash of him—

wicked, alive, young under all the violence and family ruin—struck her with more force than the kiss had.

"It does," she whispered.

His expression changed. Not much. Enough. Juliet reached behind her without looking away from him and found the small brass latch. It slid into place with a soft click that sounded indecently loud in the holy dark. Romeo's eyes dropped to her mouth.

"That may be the least Catholic sound I've ever heard," he said.

"Then you haven't been listening closely."

He kissed her again. This time there was no elegance in it. No careful beginning, no polite testing of restraint. Juliet's back hit the narrow wooden wall of the confessional, and Romeo followed, one hand braced beside her head, the other at her waist, pulling her close enough that the entire small space became heat, breath, and the simple fact of their bodies fitting where the room had no intention of allowing it. She caught the front of his coat and dragged him harder against her. He groaned into her mouth. The sound went through her like a struck match.

"Quiet," she whispered.

"You first."

She almost laughed, but his mouth found her throat and the laugh became something softer, lower, more reckless. Romeo kissed the line beneath her jaw, the pulse at her neck, the place just below her ear that made her fingers tighten in his hair. She tilted her head back against the wood, eyes closing despite herself.

"This is terrible," she breathed.

"Yes."

"Wrong."

"Yes."

"Possibly unforgivable."

His mouth moved against her skin. "Then we should make it worth confessing."

Juliet faltered. She pulled him back to her mouth. The kiss turned hungry enough to frighten her, though not enough to stop. His hand slid from her waist to her ribs, then higher, pausing at the curve of her breast as if some last civilized piece of him still meant to ask permission. Juliet covered his hand with hers and pressed it there. Romeo froze for half a breath. Then his palm closed over her through the silk.

The touch was firm, careful only until she arched into it. His thumb moved once, then again, learning what made her breath break. The confessional suddenly felt smaller than any room had a right to be. The carved wood pressed into her back. His body pressed into her front. Her own hands moved without the slightest loyalty to good sense—over his shoulders, beneath his coat, down the firm line of his stomach until he caught her wrist with a quick inhale.

"Juliet."

"Don't sound wounded. I haven't even done anything yet."

His eyes darkened.

"That," he said, "is exactly the problem."

She glanced between them, then back up. For a reckless second, she let her body answer before her mouth did, rolling against him just enough to feel the restraint leave him in a rough breath. Romeo's hand tightened at her waist. His forehead dropped briefly to hers.

"God help me," he muttered.

"This seems an unfortunate place to ask."

That broke a laugh out of him, low and disbelieving, and Juliet loved the sound so fiercely it scared her more than his hand on her breast had. Then he kissed her again, and the laughter vanished.

He lifted her slightly, not enough to be graceful, just enough that she ended up half-seated against the narrow ledge built into the booth, her skirt caught between them, one knee brushing his hip. The position was awkward and perfect. Her fingers went to his collar, tugging it open. He bent to her again, his mouth hot at her throat, his hand sliding over her thigh before stopping with visible effort. She felt that effort. Felt the tremor of it in him.

"You're trying very hard to be honorable," she whispered.

"I'm failing."

"Not enough."

His eyes lifted to hers. The look in them almost undid her. Then a cough came from somewhere outside the confessional. Both of them froze. Father Lawrence. Juliet shut her eyes. Romeo held still, except for the quick rise and fall of his chest. A second cough followed, sharper this time. Then Father Lawrence's voice came from the other side of the wood, low and lethal.

"I am beginning to suspect neither of you is using this sacrament correctly."

Juliet pressed one hand over her mouth. Romeo dropped his forehead against her shoulder.

"Do not laugh," he whispered.

"I'm trying not to."

"You're shaking."

"That is not only laughter."

His hand flexed once at her waist before he forced himself to step back. The absence of him was immediate and insulting.

Outside, Father Lawrence said, "Back where I left you. Now."

Romeo turned to Juliet. His hair was disordered, his mouth swollen, his collar open where she had pulled at it. She was sure she looked worse. Or better. That was the problem.

"I want to see you tonight," he said.

The urgency in it cut straight through the heat. Juliet stilled.

"Tonight?"

"Yes."

"Romeo—"

"I know. I know all the reasons."

"No, you don't." She reached for his shirtfront and pulled him close one last time, not for kissing now, but to make him listen. "If you come near my house, you die. If you send a car, they trace it. If you send a note, they read it."

"Then where?"

She thought fast. Her world had become corridors, guards, mother, father, Paris, Tybalt, Galina, and lies. But there were still places the house considered beneath suspicion. Ordinary places. Places powerful people did not bother imagining unless money passed through them.

"The waterfront," she whispered. "The old diner near the canal stairs. The one with the red sign."

His attention snapped into focus. "You know it?"

"I know where it is."

"That isn't the same thing."

"I'm learning quickly."

A reluctant smile touched his mouth.

"Ten," she said. "If I can get out. If I don't come by ten-thirty, leave."

"No."

"Romeo."

"No."

She gave him a look cutting enough to cut through what remained of the moment. "If I don't come by ten-thirty, it means I couldn't get free. If you wait, you become evidence. If you become evidence, I become a prisoner."

He nodded once, though he hated the idea of leaving her. "Ten," he said.

She smiled and nodded toward him. “Canal stairs. Red sign.”

Father Lawrence knocked once against the wood.

“I am seconds away from becoming extremely unpastoral.”

Juliet slipped out of Romeo’s grasp, fixed the neckline of her dress with unsteady hands, and smoothed her hair by touch alone. Romeo reached for the latch, but she caught his hand first. One last kiss. Brief. Not gentle. A promise made with mouths because words had become too slow. Then she slipped back into the left penitent stall.

Romeo disappeared into the opposite shadow just as Father Lawrence opened the center door and resumed his place with the rigid dignity of a man regretting every mercy he had ever extended. He looked once toward Juliet. Then toward Romeo. Then up at the confessional ceiling.

“I am not asking,” he said.

“That seems wise,” Juliet said, trying to sound composed.

“It seems late.”

He slid open Juliet’s screen. His voice lifted, pitched just loud enough for anyone nearby to hear the rhythm of ordinary confession without the content.

“For your penance,” Father Lawrence said, “you will reflect seriously on restraint.”

Juliet lowered her eyes. “Yes, Father.”

“And the value of timing.”

“Yes, Father.”

“And the Lord’s patience, which is not infinite, despite what certain people seem determined to test.”

From the other side of the booth, Romeo made the mistake of breathing almost like a laugh. Father Lawrence shut Juliet’s screen with unnecessary force. A moment later, Galina opened the outer door. Juliet stepped out. Galina’s eyes moved over her once. Only once. That was enough.

The loosened hair near Juliet’s temple. The flush at her throat. The mouth she had not quite managed to compose. The neckline that sat a fraction lower than it had when she entered. Galina’s expression did not change so much as sharpen into something that could have stripped varnish from wood.

“Confession was thorough,” Galina said.

Juliet lifted her chin. “Spiritually helpful.”

“I can see that.”

Father Lawrence emerged from the center compartment with the face of a man who had chosen restraint for reasons of blood pressure. Galina regarded him. He glanced over his shoulder. Whatever passed between them was old, fond, and deeply annoyed.

"Come," Galina said to Juliet. "Before you achieve further holiness."

Juliet did not look back until she reached the end of the side aisle. She should not have. Romeo was still hidden in the confessional shadow, watching her through the carved dark. Her pulse leapt like a guilty thing. Then Galina's hand closed around her elbow.

"Do not," Galina said softly.

Juliet faced forward. They left through the side door, where the Kapulet guard straightened too quickly and pretended not to have been bored. Inside the church, Romeo waited. One minute. Two. Three. Then Father Lawrence opened the opposite penitent door. Romeo stepped out, still buttoning his coat. The priest glanced at his collar. Then his mouth. Then the misfastened button on his shirt. Without warning, Father Lawrence smacked him lightly on the back of the head.

Romeo winced. "Ow."

"That was for the church."

Romeo stared at him.

Father Lawrence raised one finger. "The next one is for me."

"I thought you weren't asking."

"I did not ask because I am neither blind nor stupid." The priest pointed toward the side door. "I gave you a narrow channel of communication, not a honeymoon suite with mahogany paneling."

Romeo tried and failed not to smile.

Father Lawrence's gaze narrowed. "Do not look pleased with yourself. It makes me want to revisit what Mercutio so absurdly called practical theology."

"I'm sorry."

"No, you are not."

Romeo's smile faded, but the heat of what had happened had not left his face. Neither had the fear.

"I'm seeing her tonight."

Father Lawrence closed his eyes once.

"Of course you are."

"The waterfront. The old diner by the canal stairs. Ten."

The priest opened his eyes again. "That is reckless."

"Yes."

"Reckless."

"Yes."

"Likely to make every careful thing Galina and I have done feel personally insulted."

Romeo did not answer. Father Lawrence sighed.

"Go out through the sacristy. Not the front. Not the side aisle. And for the love of all saints, fix your shirt before you pass the Virgin."

Romeo glanced down and saw the button. For a second, he looked almost young. Father Lawrence saw it and softened only by the smallest degree. Then he pointed again.

"Go."

Romeo went. At the sacristy door, he paused. Father Lawrence stood beneath the low church light, old and irritated and worried enough to look almost angry.

"Romeo."

"Yes?"

"This feeling you have does not make you invulnerable."

Romeo's hand tightened once on the doorframe.

"No," he said. "But she makes everything else feel possible."

Father Lawrence had no answer to that. Because the boy was wrong. And because the boy was right. Romeo slipped out through the sacristy, leaving Father Lawrence alone in the old church with wax, wood, and the lingering suspicion that God had a cruel sense of timing.

Chapter 15. Wednesday Afternoon — Outside a Coffeehouse Near St. Ignatius Parish, Georgetown

Benvolio came out of the coffeehouse with his phone still in his hand and Escalus's voice still in his ear. Mercutio followed him onto the sidewalk, carrying a coffee he did not intend to finish.

"Well?" Mercutio asked.

Benvolio checked the street before answering. Habit. Nerves. Training. All three had begun to feel the same. "Escalus wants peace."

Mercutio made a soft, humorless sound. "A lovely wish. Has he considered asking the weather not to rain?"

A delivery truck groaned past them, too large for the narrow Georgetown street. Benvolio waited until the sound faded before he continued. "If anything happens publicly, Escalus burns both houses down in court."

Benvolio did not smile. "Romeo needs to stay out of sight."

Mercutio glanced toward the church end of the block. "A prudent idea. Unfortunately, the fair and beautiful Juliet appears to have struck him somewhere vital."

"That is exactly what worries me."

A black SUV rolled slowly through the intersection, paused, then kept going. Benvolio watched it until it turned.

Mercutio's lightness thinned. "You think Tybalt is coming."

"Absolutely. The note was just the beginning. He wants Romeo afraid. That's Tybalt's M.O."

Mercutio sipped his coffee and grimaced. "Terrible. Both the coffee and the man."

Benvolio's phone buzzed once. He glanced down. A text from one of his federal contacts: Kapulet detail seen near Wisconsin Ave. Tybalt likely mobile.

Benvolio put the phone away. "We need to move."

Mercutio looked past him. "Too late."

Tybalt Kapulet stood at the far corner with two men behind him. He wore a dark coat and gloves, his face composed in that polished, bloodless way that always made Benvolio think of knives wrapped in silk. He did not hurry. He did not have to. People on the sidewalk began moving aside before they understood why.

Benvolio stepped forward. "Tybalt."

"Agent Omerti."

Mercutio smiled. "And here I thought the day would be boring."

Tybalt barely acknowledged him. His eyes remained on Benvolio. "I'm looking for Romeo Montague."

"Then write another letter," Mercutio said. "Your first one was touching. Such concern for his welfare."

Tybalt's gaze shifted to him. "You should talk less."

"And deprive you of an opportunity to practice your skills?"

Benvolio cut in. "Walk away, Tybalt."

"Is that official?"

"It can be."

Tybalt's mouth moved into something that was not quite a smile. "I only want to ask him a question. I do hope he is well."

"No," Benvolio said. "Let's stop pretending, shall we? You delivered a threat to the Montague house disguised as concern."

Tybalt took one slow step closer. "A Montague came into my uncle's house. He danced with Juliet. Then blood spilled under that same roof." His eyes sharpened. "I am allowed some concern and a bit of curiosity as to how, shall we say, a pattern of coincidences occurred."

"He was not involved. The Montagues were not involved last night. Romeo owes you nothing," Benvolio said.

Tybalt's two men spread slightly behind him, not enough for anyone passing by to call it a formation, but enough for Benvolio to feel the street tighten. Mercutio noticed too, and the coffee cup lowered in his hand. Then Romeo appeared at the end of the block.

He came from the church side, though not close enough for Tybalt to know where he had been. His hair was wind-touched, his coat buttoned crookedly at the throat, and there was a brightness in him that did not belong to the hour. He looked bruised, tired, and somehow alive in a way Benvolio had not seen since before Rosaline died. Benvolio saw it and thought, Is he grinning? My God, the man is walking into a standoff grinning like a fool.

Romeo stopped beside them. His eyes moved from Benvolio to Mercutio, then to Tybalt. He seemed almost happy, and the look perplexed Tybalt. Is this man touched? Is he insane? Tybalt would have known what to do with anger. Fear would have pleased him. Romeo gave him neither. Instead, he stood there grinning, pleased with himself and the world.

"Tybalt," Romeo said.

"Montague."

"I heard you were asking for me."

"You heard correctly."

Romeo nodded once. "Then here I am."

Mercutio turned to Benvolio. "This is already unbearable."

Tybalt stepped closer. "You were in my uncle's house."

"Yes."

"You put your hands on Juliet."

Romeo's expression shifted, only slightly, but Tybalt caught it.

"You danced with her," Tybalt said. "In front of her family. In front of me."

"I did."

"And now you stand there like you have nothing to answer for."

Romeo met his eyes. "I have no quarrel with you."

The words landed badly.

Mercutio turned sharply. "What?"

Tybalt stared at Romeo as if insult had arrived in a language he disliked. "No quarrel?"

"No."

"After last night?"

Romeo's voice remained quiet. "Especially after last night."

Tybalt's smile sharpened. "So you are a coward."

Romeo did not rise to it, and that made Tybalt angrier than any insult would have.

Benvolio stepped between them. "Enough."

Tybalt ignored him. "You came into a Kapulet house under a mask. You danced with a Kapulet daughter. Men died before dawn. And now you want peace?"

Romeo's expression tightened. "I want no more killing."

Mercutio swore under his breath.

Tybalt laughed once, soft and ugly. "How noble."

Romeo did not answer.

Mercutio moved then, stepping around Benvolio and into Tybalt's line. "He said he does not want to fight you."

Tybalt regarded him. "I heard."

"Then be grateful. This is the most generous act you'll receive today."

A hard edge entered Mercutio's voice. All playful banter was gone. Benvolio reached for his sleeve.

"Don't."

Mercutio shook him off without looking back.

Tybalt's eyes narrowed. "This isn't your fight."

"No," Mercutio said. "That's why the act makes it generous."

Romeo stepped toward him. "Mercutio."

"No." Mercutio's voice stayed light, but his face had gone hard. "He came hunting you in the street because he didn't get to finish his tantrum in the ballroom. He has no intention of letting you leave again."

Tybalt smirked and pulled off one black leather glove. Benvolio saw the motion and felt the old courthouse memory flash cold through him.

"Tybalt," he warned.

Tybalt handed the glove to one of his men.

Mercutio smiled. "Very dramatic. Do you also faint in operas?"

The knife appeared low in Tybalt's hand. Not high. Not theatrical. Fast.

Benvolio's hand went to his sidearm. "Federal agent. Drop it."

One of Tybalt's men drew. The street exploded. The first shot cracked past Benvolio's shoulder and punched into the coffeehouse window. Glass burst inward. People screamed. Benvolio drew and fired back, driving the man behind a parked sedan. The second Kapulet man pulled a gun near the curb. Benvolio swung toward him.

"Drop it!"

The man fired instead. Benvolio dropped behind a newspaper box as the round tore through the metal edge. He returned fire once, twice. The second man stumbled backward, then ducked behind a delivery van. Car alarms started screaming. Mercutio and Tybalt were already in close.

Tybalt lunged with the knife. Mercutio caught his wrist, twisted inside the slash, and drove his elbow into Tybalt's ribs. Tybalt staggered, recovered, and came again. Mercutio was faster than he looked. He moved with reckless, precise grace, anger lending shape to every strike. He caught Tybalt across the mouth, then drove him backward against the side of a parked SUV. Tybalt slashed and caught only cloth. Mercutio trapped the knife wrist against the hood and struck him again. For a clean instant, Mercutio had him. Benvolio saw it from behind the newspaper box. Romeo saw it too.

"Mercutio, stop!"

Mercutio did not look away from Tybalt. "I have him."

Romeo stepped in anyway. Not to save Tybalt. Not to betray Mercutio. To stop the knife, the gunfire, the bloodshed spreading through a public street. He caught Mercutio by the shoulder and shoved between them.

"Stop. Both of you."

Mercutio turned, furious. “Romeo, let go!”

Tybalt took the opening. He wrenched his wrist free and drove the knife forward into Mercutio’s ribs. The blade disappeared. For a second, no one understood. Mercutio glanced at the wound as if it had offended him. Then Tybalt pulled the knife free, and Romeo caught Mercutio before he fell.

“No.”

Mercutio’s hand went to his side. When it came away slick with blood, his expression changed. Disbelief first. Then anger.

“Oh,” he said, and coughed once. “That’s rude.”

Benvolio saw his friend and screamed for him. Another shot cracked. He turned and fired again, forcing Tybalt’s man back into cover as sirens began somewhere distant.

Romeo lowered Mercutio to the pavement and pressed both hands over the wound. There was too much blood. It was immediate, hot, and very dark, pushing through his fingers before he could seal anything.

“Stay with me,” Romeo ordered.

Mercutio focused on him. “You sound terrible,” he gasped.

“Shut up.”

“That’s better.” Mercutio coughed again, and blood touched his lips.

Romeo froze. The sound changed him. Whatever softness had carried him from Juliet, whatever light the church had left in him, vanished. Tybalt stepped backward, knife still in hand. Romeo turned to him.

“Romeo,” Benvolio warned as more shots rang out.

Romeo stood. Mercutio’s life was on his hands.

“Romeo,” Benvolio shouted again.

But Romeo had already gone somewhere words could not reach. Tybalt recognized something in Romeo’s face. It was not the face of a sane man; there was an intensity that burned in his stance, his face, and his eyes. Tybalt turned as if to leave. Romeo lunged.

They hit the side of the SUV hard enough to dent metal. Tybalt slashed. Romeo caught his wrist with both hands and slammed it against the hood once, twice, until the knife dropped and skidded beneath the car. Tybalt punched him in the jaw. Romeo hit him back with raw savagery.

There was no grace or polish in the fight. It was intense and one-sided. Tybalt’s defenses failed him under the brute force, the abandonment of Romeo’s own safety in his attack, and the pure carelessness of his rage.

More rounds from the two Kapulet men continued to pin Benvolio down behind his cover. He screamed for Romeo, trying to get through to him, trying to stop him.

"Romeo, stop!"

Tybalt drove a knee into Romeo's ribs and shoved him back toward the curb. Romeo stumbled. Tybalt grabbed a loose brick from the broken edge of the sidewalk and swung. Romeo ducked just enough that it grazed his head, and they went down together onto the curb. The brick hit the pavement between them. Romeo reached it first.

Benvolio saw the movement and screamed, "No!"

Romeo rose over Tybalt with the brick in his hand, and for the first time, Tybalt looked afraid. Romeo brought the brick down. Once. The sound was small, but final. Tybalt's body jerked, then went slack. The street froze as eyes turned to the scene. Then the sirens screamed closer, swallowing everything.

Tybalt's men ran. One limped toward the alley. The other vanished behind the delivery van. Benvolio peered out, aghast at the scene, then surged toward Mercutio, his hands coming to the wound. Romeo stared down at Tybalt. The brick slipped from his hand and hit the street. Mercutio coughed.

Romeo turned and stumbled back to him. "Mercutio."

Mercutio fixed on him with eyes bright from pain and fury.

"You saved him," Mercutio whispered.

Romeo shook his head. "No."

"I had him."

"I was trying to stop it."

"You stopped me," his raspy voice continued. "You killed me."

The rage that overwhelmed Romeo evaporated, and he went white.

Benvolio pressed harder against the wound. "Stay with me."

"Bossy," Mercutio breathed.

"You can insult me later."

"Can't promise later."

Blue and red light began to flash against the coffeehouse windows. Mercutio's gaze moved past Benvolio to Tybalt's body.

"Did you kill him?" Mercutio asked.

Romeo nodded. "Yes."

"Good," he whispered.

Then his eyes found Romeo again, and the anger returned, weaker now, but sharper for being almost spent.

"Damn you."

Romeo bent over him and grasped his arm. "Mercutio—"

"Damn both your houses." His breathing faltered.

Benvolio's throat closed. Mercutio's grip tightened once on Romeo's sleeve.

"And damn you," he whispered.

Then pain took him again. His body convulsed once with a rough, wet cough. Blood ran from the corner of his mouth. His eyes fixed briefly on the gray sky between the buildings as if he had found one last thing worth mocking but no strength left to say it. His hand loosened.

Benvolio felt it happen. "No."

Mercutio did not answer.

Benvolio bent over him. "No. Mercutio. Stay with me."

Romeo sat frozen beside them. A patrol car screamed to a stop at the corner. Doors slammed. Officers shouted. Someone else called for EMTs. Benvolio looked up and saw Romeo still kneeling there, blood on his face, his hands, and his shirt. Tybalt dead ten feet away. Mercutio dead beneath Benvolio's hands. Witnesses everywhere. Reality hit him.

"Romeo."

Romeo stayed where he was.

Benvolio grabbed him by the front of the coat with one bloody hand and shook him hard. "Romeo!"

His eyes focused. Barely.

Benvolio shoved him backward. "Run."

"What?"

"Run."

"I can't leave him."

"He's gone." The words tore through Benvolio as they came. "He's gone, and if you are arrested, the Kapulets will find a way to kill you before you are booked."

Romeo turned toward Tybalt. "I killed him."

"Yes."

"I killed Juliet's cousin."

"Yes." Benvolio's voice broke into a shout.

Romeo's breathing shook.

"Find Father Lawrence," Benvolio said. "Do not go home. Do not call your father. Go to Father Lawrence, now!"

Romeo sprinted away down the alleyway just as an officer shouted behind Benvolio, "Hands where I can see them!"

Benvolio lifted one bloody hand and reached for his badge with the other. “Federal agent!” he shouted. “Federal agent! Victim down!”

Benvolio stayed on his knees as an EMT dropped beside Mercutio.

For a few frantic moments, the medic worked over him. Then he looked up and said, “He’s gone.”

Benvolio heard him. He did not understand him. Blue and red light washed over the street. Police closed in around Tybalt’s body. Someone pulled Benvolio back, but he leaned forward again, one hand still reaching for Mercutio, refusing to accept that he was gone. At the mouth of the alley, Romeo was gone. Benvolio looked down at his hands. Mercutio’s blood was sticky and already drying into the lines of his skin.

Chapter 16. Wednesday Evening — Juliet's Rooms, Kapulet Townhouse, Georgetown

Juliet heard her mother before the house told her why. It began somewhere below, not as a scream at first, but as a sound too raw to belong in Ekaterina Kapulet's body: a broken breath, a denial. Then glass shattered, and the sound became a wail that moved through the townhouse faster than any servant dared.

Juliet stood from the edge of her bed, the floor seeming to tilt slightly beneath her. Galina looked up from the tea tray, and her expression changed before the door opened.

"What is it?" Juliet asked.

Galina did not answer. The door flew open, and Ekaterina came in as if someone had struck her and left her walking. Her pearls were gone. Her hair, always pinned like discipline itself, had loosened at one temple. She looked first at Juliet, then past her, as if the room had failed to contain the person she needed most.

"Tybalt," she said.

Juliet's hands went cold. "What happened?"

Ekaterina crossed the room and caught Juliet by the shoulders. The grip was too hard, but Juliet did not pull away.

"He is dead."

The words entered her and would not settle. Tybalt. Dead. In an instant, Juliet saw him as a boy, dangerous and beautiful and already cruel, teaching her how to hold a knife because he said pretty girls were the first ones men underestimated. She saw him in the ballroom, fury swallowed under Viktor's command. She saw him in the corridor after the attack, eyes looking for someone to punish. Dead did not fit him.

"No," Juliet whispered.

"Yes." Ekaterina's mouth shook. "Romeo Montague killed him." She spoke Montague with venom.

Juliet stepped back, and Ekaterina saw it. Pain sharpened into accusation before Juliet had time to hide herself.

"You knew him," her mother said, her tone edged with betrayal.

Juliet froze. "What?"

"The Montague boy."

Juliet's confusion came honestly at first. For a terrifying instant, she thought her mother knew everything—the cellar, the church, the locked confessional door, the canal stairs waiting later in the dark. Then Ekaterina's face collapsed and hardened again.

"You danced with him," she said accusingly. "In our house. In front of everyone. In front of Tybalt."

Juliet could not answer quickly enough, and her mother mistook the hesitation for guilt of a smaller kind.

"Your cousin is dead," Ekaterina said. "Dead in the street. By that boy's hands."

"What happened?" Juliet asked. "No—tell me what happened. All of it. Not just his name at the end."

Ekaterina stared at her, then laughed once, a terrible sound. "Not just his name at the end?"

"Mother—"

"His friend died first." Ekaterina's voice cut and broke at once. "Mercutio Vale. Tybalt stabbed him. Then Romeo killed Tybalt."

Mercutio. Juliet saw his face from the masquerade only in fragments: quick smile, bright eyes, a man who seemed to thrive in danger with his wit. Romeo's friend. Romeo had watched his friend die, then killed Juliet's cousin. The pain inside her split and turned against itself.

Ekaterina drew her close suddenly, and Juliet let her. For a brief span they stood almost like mother and daughter in the old sense, before arrangements and Paris and Romeos had made love into something with conditions. Ekaterina's body shook once. Juliet's arms came around her because Tybalt had been family, because her mother had loved him in ways she rarely admitted, because death was still death. Then Ekaterina pulled away.

"All of this," she said, wiping at her face with the back of her hand as if rage were more acceptable than tears, "all of this began when he entered our house."

Juliet shook her head, still trying to make the pieces fit. "No. That can't be the whole of it."

"The whole of what?"

"Tybalt killed his friend," Juliet said. "You said that."

Ekaterina's face hardened. "And Romeo Montague killed my nephew, your cousin."

"I know." Juliet's voice broke on the last word. "I know, but why did Tybalt go looking for him at all?"

"Because Romeo had no business in our house."

"He danced with me," Juliet said, the words coming out almost bewildered. "That is not enough reason for two men to die in the street."

Ekaterina stared at her as if the sentence itself were disloyal. "You will not leave these rooms tonight. You will not ask for church. You will not ask for air. And you will not speak as if a dance with a Montague has made you innocent of what has happened to Tybalt. You may not have stabbed Tybalt, but you are complicit in this affair."

Juliet stayed quiet.

"Do you understand me?"

"Yes."

The answer sounded obedient enough to satisfy a woman too wounded to inspect it.

Ekaterina turned toward Galina. "She takes the sleeping medicine. The doctor left it after the attack. She needs rest."

Galina inclined her head once. "Yes, madam."

Ekaterina turned back to Juliet, and for one moment her face almost softened. Almost.

"Tybalt is dead," she said, as if saying it again might finally make the room accept it. "And I have to tell your father that his daughter defends the boy who killed him."

Then she left, and the door shut behind her. Juliet stood very still. Galina crossed to the tea tray and poured water into a small glass. Beside it waited the amber bottle the house doctor had sent up that morning: mild sedative, he had said. For shock. For sleep. For young women who had seen too much and were still expected to wake presentable. Galina measured the dose while Juliet watched.

"You should ask me what I know," Juliet said.

Galina did not look up. "I know enough."

"No, you don't."

The older woman set the bottle down. "Then tell me what you can afford to say."

Juliet's throat tightened. She could not say: I am supposed to meet him tonight. She could not say: He asked if the confessional door locked, and I wanted him badly enough to forget where we were. She could not say: At ten, by the canal stairs, under the red sign, if the world has not ended first.

So she said, "Do you think she's right? That I should hate him?"

Galina came to her slowly. "I think hatred is very useful to people who do not wish to think."

Juliet let out a breath that nearly became a sob. "He killed Tybalt."

"Yes."

"His friend died first."

"Yes."

"And I—" She pressed one hand firmly against her mouth, hating herself for the truth forming beneath it. "I am more afraid for Romeo than I am angry for Tybalt."

Galina's face did not flinch, and that mercy nearly broke her.

"I'm monstrous," Juliet whispered.

"No," Galina said. "You are alive, and the living are not tidy."

Juliet turned toward the window. Georgetown had gone dark beyond the glass. Somewhere beyond those streets Romeo was hidden, arrested, wounded, fleeing, or alone with Mercutio's blood on him. He might think she hated him. He might be right to.

Galina touched her shoulder. "You loved Tybalt in the way children love what frightens and protects them at once. That kind of mourning is never clean."

"And Romeo?"

Galina's hand fell away. "That," she said carefully, "is the part you must not let decide everything tonight."

Juliet closed her eyes. Tonight. The word struck like a bell.

Galina lifted the glass with the sleeping medicine dissolved clear inside it. "Drink. Sleep if you can. Morning will be uglier if you meet it hollow."

Juliet stared at the glass. If she drank, she would sleep. She would not go to the canal stairs. She would not see Romeo. She would not have to decide whether mourning changed love into betrayal. If she did not drink, she would walk into the night toward a man who had killed her cousin and lost his friend because of her world, his world, and the fragile place where the two had touched. The clock on the mantel clicked toward nine. Galina held out the glass. Juliet reached for it, her fingers closing around the rim as she peered into it, lost in thought.

Chapter 17. Wednesday Night — Rectory Rooms, St. Ignatius Parish, Georgetown

Romeo had stopped shaking by the time Father Lawrence found him in the old rectory room. That worried the priest more than if he had been weeping. Men who shook could still be brought back to their bodies. Men who stilled too early had often gone somewhere language could not easily follow.

Romeo sat in a chair near the narrow window, coat open, shirt stained at the cuff, hands hanging loose between his knees. Father Lawrence had made him wash once, then twice, then had taken the towel away when Romeo kept scrubbing as if water could reach what he had done. The blood had left his skin. It had not left his eyes.

Father Lawrence shut the door behind him. "Benvolio is alive."

Romeo looked up at once.

"He stayed at the scene. Police have him. Escalus is there. No one has named this cleanly yet, which means there is still room to keep you alive."

Romeo's mouth moved. "Mercutio?"

The priest did not soften his face.

"No."

The word entered the room and stayed. Romeo looked back down at his hands.

"I killed Tybalt."

"Yes."

"I killed Juliet's cousin."

"Yes."

Father Lawrence crossed to the small table and poured water into a chipped glass. "And if I hear you say it a third time, as if repetition is confession, I may lose patience."

Romeo's eyes lifted, hollow and furious. "What would you have me call it?"

"Consequence," Father Lawrence said. "Tragedy. Rage. A sin born out of another sin. Many words fit. None of them return the dead."

Romeo stood too fast. "He killed Mercutio."

"Yes."

"I tried to stop it."

"Yes."

"I made the opening."

Father Lawrence's expression tightened. That was the wound, then. Not only Tybalt dead. Not only Mercutio. Romeo had found the place where his own intention had failed and made a grave of it.

The priest set the glass down. "Sit."

"No."

"Romeo."

"No." He pressed one hand against the window frame and looked out toward the dark churchyard. "I can't sit in this room while she hears what I did."

"She may already have heard."

The words nearly bent him.

Romeo closed his eyes once. "Then she hates me."

"You do not know that."

"I killed her kin."

"After her kin killed your childhood friend."

Romeo turned sharply. "It does not balance my sins."

"It does not." Father Lawrence's voice hardened. "I am keeping you from walking down the dangerous road with your eyes closed. Tybalt chose violence. Mercutio chose to defend you. You chose to stop them, and then you chose revenge. None of that makes you innocent. None of it makes you the only guilty man, either. Grief will try to tell you otherwise. It will turn one death into the reason for the next, one mistake into the end of mercy, and one wound into permission for the whole city to bleed."

Romeo's breathing shook.

The priest lowered his voice. "Listen to me. There is a man outside watching the parish gate. One of Benvolio's people. If Kapulet security comes near, he sends word. If Montague men come near, he sends word. You are not leaving through the front, and you are not going home."

Romeo did not answer.

"Tomorrow morning, just before dawn, Brother John will take you to a handoff beyond the District line. From there, another car will carry you west. There is a safe house in the mountains near Cumberland. Old parish property. No phones or emails tied to your family, or even to me. The police know who I am, and they are watching. Everything will be handled by courier. I will send word to your father, and he will send someone to us. You will stay there until Escalus decides whether the city wants law or vengeance more."

"Exile," Romeo said.

"Survival."

"They are the same tonight."

"No," Father Lawrence said. "Only to men young enough to think every closed door is death."

Romeo almost laughed. It came out broken. He thought of the diner. The canal stairs. The red sign. Ten o'clock. He had not told Father Lawrence. He could not tell him now.

If he said Juliet had asked him to meet her, the priest would stop him. Worse, he would be right to try. Juliet had every reason not to come. Every reason to hate him, to sleep, to grieve Tybalt, to let the night close over whatever tenderness had existed in a confessional before the street took lives from both houses. But if she went there and he did not—No. That thought hurt worse than exile.

Father Lawrence watched him too closely. "What are you not saying?"

Romeo faced him. Nothing. The pause was its own lie.

The priest sighed. "Do not make me guess. I am old and usually correct."

"There's nothing."

"Then you are lying badly on church property. That offends me professionally."

Romeo picked up the glass and drank because it gave him three seconds not to answer. Father Lawrence let him have them.

Then he said, "If this is about Juliet, you do nothing tonight."

Romeo's hand tightened around the glass.

"There it is," the priest said.

Romeo set the glass down carefully. "You don't understand."

"I understand more than you want me to."

"No." Romeo's voice went rough. "If I disappear before she sees me, then all she has is the story other people tell. Tybalt dead. Mercutio dead. Romeo gone. That becomes the truth because I was not there to bear it in front of her."

"You think appearing before a grieving girl will heal what happened?"

"No."

"Then what?"

Romeo turned toward the window again. The glass reflected him dimly: bruised, hollow-eyed, alive when Mercutio was not.

"I would rather be judged by her than forgiven by everyone else."

Father Lawrence stayed quiet.

"I don't expect mercy," Romeo continued. "I don't expect her to come. I don't expect anything. But if there is one chance she stands in the cold waiting for me, and I am not there—" His voice failed, then returned lower. "Then whatever is left of me deserves exile."

The priest closed his eyes briefly. When he opened them, the burden had made him older.

"This is exactly how young men die."

"I know."

"No," Father Lawrence said. "You don't. You have seen death. That is not the same as understanding how eagerly it accepts invitations."

Romeo almost smiled, though not quite. "You are very bad at comfort."

"I was not attempting it."

A knock sounded below.

Father Lawrence crossed to the door, opened it, listened, then came back. "The watcher says the street is clear for now. That will not hold all night."

Romeo nodded.

"Good," Father Lawrence said. "Then hear me plainly. At six-thirty, you leave this rectory with Brother John. You do not argue. You do not make Benvolio choose between the Bureau and burying another man he loves. You do not let Mercutio's death become the excuse for your own."

Romeo flinched. The priest regretted the sharpness, but not enough to withdraw it.

"Do you understand?"

"Yes."

"Say it."

"At six-thirty, I leave."

Father Lawrence regarded him. Romeo held his gaze. It was not enough. But the priest had no proof, and the night had already taken more than proof could manage.

At last Father Lawrence stepped back. "Try to sleep."

Romeo turned to him.

The priest gave a tired, humorless breath. "Fine. Sit in the dark and contemplate ruin. It seems to be the fashion."

He left Romeo alone. For several minutes, Romeo remained where he was. He remembered Juliet's words: Canal stairs. Red sign. Ten. Juliet would not come, but what if she did? This would be his last opportunity to see her. To be judged by her.

His life, as he had known it, was finished. By dawn he would be smuggled out of D.C. like a hunted thing. By morning, every person who loved him would have a reason to regret it. But ten o'clock existed before dawn. Romeo stood, took Father Lawrence's black coat from the chair, and listened for footsteps in the hall. There were none. He opened the window.

Chapter 18. Wednesday Night — Canal Stairs Near the Red Sign, Georgetown

The red sign buzzed over the canal like a tired star. Half of its letters had burned low enough to turn the diner's sign into something almost unreadable, a crooked wash of red light trembling over wet pavement, dark windows, and the narrow stairs that led down toward the old water. Georgetown had gone cold after the rain. Brick held the damp. The railing shone black. Somewhere beneath the street, the canal moved without sound, carrying reflections in broken strips of red and gold. Romeo stood in the shadow beside the stairs, wearing Father Lawrence's black coat.

It was too broad in the shoulders and too long at the cuffs. It smelled faintly of wool, smoke, and church incense. He had taken it because it hid what memory left even after the fabric had been washed, because it made him less immediately recognizable, because he had needed something not his own around him when he climbed out of the rectory window and walked toward the only hour left before exile. Ten o'clock came. Then slipped past by one minute. Then two. The stairs above the canal remained empty.

Romeo told himself that was better. Juliet should be behind locked doors, grieving Tybalt, protected by Galina, far from him and everything his family had brought into her life. She should let the house keep her tonight. She should sleep if she could. She should wake in the morning having chosen herself over a man who would be gone before dawn. She should hate him. He told himself that too, though the thought cut deeper each time he reached for it.

If she stayed away, he could carry her judgment without protest. If she came, he would have to look her in the eyes and learn whether love could survive what his hands had done. He did not know which possibility frightened him more. Then he heard footsteps above the stairs. Romeo lifted his head. Juliet appeared under the red sign.

At first, she was only silhouette and motion, a dark coat buttoned to her throat, hair loosened by weather and haste, face pale under the neon. Then she saw him. Everything in her broke at once.

She came down the steps too quickly, one hand catching the rail, the other pressed firmly against her chest as if she had been holding herself together by force and had lost the strength for it now that he was real. Romeo moved toward her. They met halfway.

Juliet rushed into his arms, both arms locking around his neck, and Romeo caught her so tightly she made a small, broken sound against his shoulder. Not pain. Relief. Something torn out of her before pride could stop it. He buried his face in her hair and held on as if the city might still take her if his grip loosened. She was shaking. So was he. For several breaths neither spoke.

The world narrowed to the cold stone steps, the red light above them, Juliet's fingers digging into his coat, Romeo's mouth pressed to her hair, both of them alive when so much of the day had taught them that living was temporary and badly defended. Then Juliet pulled back just enough to see him. Her hands went to his face.

The bruise at his jaw. The cut at his mouth. The swollen mark at his temple where the brick had grazed him. She touched each one as if touch could measure the truth her house had denied her. Romeo stayed where he was. Her eyes filled. Tears spilled before she could turn away.

"You came," she whispered.

He almost broke at that. "I thought you wouldn't." His voice roughened. "I thought you'd hate me."

Juliet shook her head once, hard enough that the tears fell faster.

"I tried."

The words hurt more than accusation would have. Romeo closed his eyes.

Juliet's thumb brushed the split at his mouth. "I couldn't."

He caught her wrist and pressed his lips to the inside of it. A desperate, reverent touch. Her pulse jumped. The pulse under his mouth beat quick and alive. Then she kissed him. There was nothing careful in it.

No priest outside the door. No confessional screen. No time purchased in minutes by Galina's discipline. The kiss was grief, hunger, and forgiveness arriving before either of them had earned or understood it. Juliet clutched at him as if she meant to climb inside his coat and hide there from the whole city. Romeo's hands found her back, her waist, the cold curve of her cheek, unable to decide where to hold because all of her seemed necessary. She tasted like tears. He kissed them from her mouth.

She made a broken sound, and he answered it with his whole body, backing her into the shadow beside the stair where the red sign flickered over them in pulses. Her hands slid beneath the priest's coat and found him through his shirt, warm and shaking. His fingers tightened at her waist. Her body pressed against his so completely that the cold left him in one rush. The whole city briefly disappeared. Then Juliet drew back, breathing heavily. Her eyes moved once toward the street above. Toward the diner window. Toward the narrow mouth of the alley beyond the canal stairs. Decision, not hesitation, came into her face. She took his hand.

Romeo glanced at their joined fingers, then back at her. Juliet did not explain. She led him up from the canal and across the wet sidewalk, past the diner and the red sign, past an alley where steam rose from a grate, past two hotel awnings glowing amber against the dark. She walked quickly, head lowered, coat collar lifted, her hand locked around his as if the night itself had become a corridor and she had chosen the door.

The hotel near the corner was old enough to look respectable and small enough to be forgotten. Juliet had reserved the room under an alias no one in her house would think to search. She went through the side entrance without slowing. Romeo followed. No one stopped them. No one called after them. In the elevator, Juliet leaned back against the brass wall and watched him. The doors closed. They were alone. For a suspended moment, they only stared at each other, both breathing too hard for calm. Then Romeo crossed the small space and kissed her again.

Juliet caught him by the lapels of Father Lawrence's coat and pulled him down to her mouth. His body covered hers against the elevator wall. Her hands went into his hair. His hand slid beneath her coat to her waist, then higher along her ribs, feeling the shape of her through wool and silk and the tremor beneath both. The elevator chimed. They broke apart only because the doors opened. Juliet took his hand again. This time, Romeo followed as if there had never been any other road. The hotel room was dim when Juliet opened the door.

A narrow room. Cream walls. Heavy curtains. One low lamp beside a bed already turned down by some anonymous hand. A window looked over the dark back street and the black line of the canal beyond it. The hotel room smelled faintly of clean linen, rain-soaked wool, and the lemon polish hotels used to make absence feel luxurious. Juliet locked the door. The click of it moved through Romeo like a final warning and an answer.

She stood with her back to the door, still in her coat, cheeks damp, mouth swollen from the stairwell and elevator, eyes fixed on him with a longing so open it made him forget how to breathe. He crossed to her slowly.

Not because he was unsure, but because if he moved too quickly, he might frighten them both with how badly he wanted to erase the space. Juliet met him halfway. This kiss began softer.

Not because there was less hunger, but because pain had made them fragile in places the body knew before the mind admitted it. Romeo touched her face, and Juliet leaned into his palm. Her eyes closed. He kissed her forehead, the bridge of her nose, the corner of her mouth. She turned and caught his lips again, and the softness tore open. Her fingers pushed the black coat from his shoulders. It fell to the floor.

Then his jacket. Then her coat. Wet wool dropped in a dark heap beside the door. Romeo's hands moved to the buttons at her throat, and Juliet stilled under the touch. Not from fear. From the intimacy of being undone slowly. He watched her. She nodded once.

His fingers worked carefully down the front of her blouse. One button. Then another. The lamplight touched the hollow of her throat, the line of her collarbone, the shadow of skin beneath fabric. Juliet's breath changed with each inch revealed. When he reached the last button, she caught his hands. He froze. Then she brought his wounded palm to her mouth.

The bandage was rough against her lips. She kissed the cloth once, then the bruised knuckles above it, then the faint place near his wrist where the blood had been and no washing would ever truly remove it. Romeo bowed his head. Juliet stepped closer and pressed his hand flat against her chest. Her heart beat beneath his palm. Alive. He watched her then with such raw gratitude that her eyes filled again. She shook her head as if refusing tears now, refusing anything but him, and pushed his shirt from his trousers. They undressed each other without speaking, the quiet broken only by breath and the small sounds of fabric giving way.

His shirt opened under her hands. Juliet saw the bruise across his ribs where Tybalt's knee had landed, the shallow cut near his shoulder, the older scar low along his side she did not know the story of yet. She touched each mark. Slowly. Reverently. Her fingertips traced violence without flinching from it. Romeo watched her face as she looked at him—not at Romeo Montague, not at the killer of Tybalt, but at the man who had come to her carrying the wreckage of a day neither of them could undo. Juliet's blouse slid from her shoulders.

Romeo's eyes moved over her, and the look itself felt like contact. Her skin warmed beneath it. He did not make her feel displayed. He made her feel discovered. The difference was so sharp she nearly trembled from it. He touched the bandage at her temple first. Then the faint bruise near her wrist where the attacker had grabbed her in the cellar. Then the small line of red at her collarbone where lace had rubbed too hard in her haste to dress. His mouth followed his hand. Juliet closed her eyes when he kissed the bruise at her wrist. When he kissed the hollow of her throat, her fingers tightened in his hair.

When his mouth moved lower, she whispered his name, and he made a sound that was almost pain. There was nothing polished left between them. No ballroom. No church. No cleverness. Only skin and breath, scars and need, the trembling work of removing every barrier the world had not yet managed to make permanent.

Juliet pushed his shirt from his shoulders. Her hands went to the belt at his waist, and Romeo caught his breath as she undid it, drew the fabric down, and exposed him fully.

Naked before her, Romeo moved his hands to her skirt, then paused. Juliet smiled faintly at the contradiction: this man who had shown no hesitation in danger now hesitated before undressing her. She guided his hands, reassuring him without words that she wanted this. When the last of their clothing fell away, they stood beside the bed in the amber light and met each other's eyes. Naked, both of them. Not safe, not innocent, not untouched by what had happened, but alive.

Romeo reached for her as if the sight of her had undone whatever restraint the day had left him. Juliet came into his arms with a small gasp, skin to skin now, heat against heat, her body fitting to his with an intimacy so immediate it felt less like discovery than return. He kissed her deeply. She answered with everything.

Her hands moved over his shoulders, down his back, across the firm line of muscle and injury. His hands found her waist, then her hips, then the soft curve of her back as he drew her against him. Juliet rose onto her toes, pressing closer, needing no language to tell him what the day had taken and what only this night could give back. They fell to the bed together. The sheets were cold at first. Then not.

Romeo braced himself above her, and for one moment the force of wanting her was so visible in him that Juliet reached up and touched his face again, grounding them both. He lowered his mouth to hers slowly.

The kiss deepened as his body settled over hers. She opened to him with a trust that made his control shudder. His hand moved along her side, over her breast, down to her hip, learning her not as conquest but as if he were learning a piece of himself. Juliet arched beneath him, breath catching as his mouth followed, as he kissed every place the day had left undefended.

He moved down her body with a patience that did not feel gentle so much as devoted. His mouth learned her throat, her shoulder, the curve of her breast, the trembling line of her stomach. Juliet's hands found the sheets, then his hair, then his shoulders again, as if she could not decide whether to hold the room together or pull him apart. Every touch deepened the heat between them. Every kiss made the world outside less believable.

When he came back to her mouth, she was flushed and breathless beneath him, her eyes dark with wanting and wet with everything that had brought them here. She touched his face again, then his chest, then lower, letting herself learn him with the same reverence he had given her. Romeo's breath broke under her hand. His control, already thin, nearly failed entirely. Juliet saw it. For the first time all night, something almost like a smile touched her mouth. Not innocence, but recognition.

She pushed him gently onto his back and followed him, her hair falling around them like a curtain. She kissed him slowly at first, then with growing hunger, her hands moving over his chest, his ribs, the bruises that made him flinch and the places that made him forget to breathe. Romeo's hands came to her waist, not forcing, only holding, as if even now he needed her to choose every inch. She did. Her body settled over his, and both of them stilled. For a suspended instant, there was only breath. Then she bent and kissed him.

Romeo's hands tightened at her hips, his face strained with restraint and wonder. Juliet's hips moved. A small movement. Then another. Romeo soon found the rhythm, both with his waist and with his hands on her hips.

Their bodies understood what their lives did not: that some forms of truth had to be built, not spoken. Juliet leaned over him, forehead near his, hair brushing his face, one hand braced against his chest, where his heart beat hard beneath her palm. Romeo rose to meet her, every movement deepening the ache, every breath carrying her name without quite shaping it.

The bed creaked. Rain touched the window. The red sign outside flickered through the curtains in faint, broken pulses, turning the walls briefly warm, then dark, then warm again. Juliet's breathing turned ragged. Romeo's hands moved from her hips and slid along her back, and then she shuddered first, overcome by ecstasy.

Not neatly. Not quietly. Her body trembled over his, and her face tightened with a pleasure so raw it looked almost like pain. Romeo pulled her down against him, held her through it, and kissed her shoulder, her throat, her mouth—wherever he could reach while she shook. For a few breaths, she stayed folded against him, trembling through the last of it, her forehead pressed to his and her hand braced over his heart.

Romeo hungered for more of her. He turned them carefully, bringing her beneath him without breaking their connection. Juliet wrapped her legs and arms around him and felt his own rhythm building. She instinctively pulled him closer, not to keep him there forever—there was no forever tonight—but to keep him there for this. One more breath. One more movement. One more stolen second when he was alive in her arms and she was not being taken from him by family, violence, dawn, or exile.

He moved with increasing urgency, but he never stopped being attentive to her. One hand braced near her head. The other held her hip. His mouth found hers again and again, kissing away the sounds that escaped her, giving her his own when he could no longer hold them back. The end came like a breaking wave.

Juliet clung to him, her body lifting to meet his as if the whole ruined day could be answered, if only briefly, by this desperate joining. Romeo followed her, shuddering hard, his face buried against her neck, her name a low, broken whisper. Then everything stilled: rain, breathing, and the faint hum of the red sign beyond the curtains.

Romeo lowered himself beside her, careful even in exhaustion, but Juliet pulled him back before distance could become habit. She wanted his weight, his warmth, the proof of him still close. He came willingly, half over her, one arm wrapped beneath her shoulders, his face turned into her hair. For a long time afterward, neither spoke. Words would have made the room smaller. Juliet pressed her mouth to Romeo's shoulder, and he turned his head enough to kiss her hair.

Outside, the city kept its own brutal counsel. Inside, the hotel room was warm, ruined, and full of them. Their clothes lay scattered across the floor like the remains of lives briefly abandoned. The sheets were tangled. Her coat and Father Lawrence's black one lay together near the door. Romeo's breathing eased against her neck. Juliet's hands moved once over his back, then stilled. There were no words clean enough yet.

Only this: two bodies made tender by violence, finding, for one night, a language older than the feud and more binding than any promise.

Chapter 19. Thursday Pre-dawn — Hotel Near the Canal, Georgetown

Romeo woke before the room did. The world beyond the curtains was still dark, but it had begun to loosen at the edges. The hour before dawn always carried a different hush, thinner than night, less merciful. In the narrow hotel room, the lamp had burned itself into a weak amber circle.

Their clothes remained where they had fallen. Juliet's coat lay over Romeo's black borrowed one beside the door. One of her shoes had tipped beneath the chair. His shirt hung half over the foot of the bed like a thing defeated. Juliet slept with one hand against his chest. Not deeply. Not peacefully. But against him.

Her hair had spilled across his shoulder. Her cheek rested over his heart. The sheet covered them both to the waist, though it had tangled low around her back and one bare shoulder remained exposed to the cool room. He watched her in the dim light and felt grief gather differently now—not less, never less, but altered by the shape of her breathing.

Mercutio was still dead. Tybalt was still dead. By six-thirty, Brother John would come for a man who was supposed to be in Father Lawrence's rectory. By dawn, Romeo would be smuggled west out of D.C. like a threat Washington hoped distance might contain.

But Juliet's hand was on his chest. For a little while longer, that fact argued with everything. She stirred before he touched her. Her fingers tightened over his heart. Then her eyes opened, slow and dark in the half-light.

"You're awake," she murmured.

"Yes." He kissed her forehead. She closed her eyes again and moved closer, as if the kiss had given her permission to deny the hour. Outside, a bird called from somewhere along the canal. Juliet stilled.

Then she said, "That is not a bird."

Romeo glanced toward the curtains.

"It sounded like one."

"No." Her voice was thick with sleep and refusal. "It's a truck brake. Or a bad hinge."

"A bad hinge with feathers?"

She lifted her head just enough to glare at him. The sight nearly broke him with tenderness. Her hair was wild, her mouth still soft from his kisses, her eyes shadowed by loss and too little rest. She looked younger in that moment, and older too, like a woman who had stepped out of the life chosen for her and found the new one waiting with a knife at its throat. Another bird answered outside.

Juliet shut her eyes. "No."

"Juliet."

"No. Dawn is not allowed."

"It rarely asks permission."

"Then it has poor manners."

He brushed hair back from her face. "I have to go."

She rolled away from him at once, not far, just enough to put her back to him and the whole force of her refusal into the space between their bodies.

"No."

Romeo turned onto his side behind her and touched her shoulder. "If I'm not back before Father Lawrence discovers I left, I am not sure what we will do. I may not be able to leave the city."

"Good. Then he can keep you here."

He kissed the bare slope of her shoulder. She trembled once but did not turn.

"Juliet."

"I hate that voice."

"What voice?"

"The one you use when you are about to be reasonable."

"I'm not being reasonable. I'm obeying the last living adult who knows where to hide me."

That made her turn. Her expression had changed.

"Where?"

He did not answer quickly enough.

"Romeo."

"Western Maryland," he said. "A safe house near Cumberland. Father Lawrence says Brother John takes me to a handoff before dawn. Another car from there. No Montague driver. No phone tied to my father."

The words entered her one by one: Western Maryland, safe house, before dawn. Distance taking shape as geography.

Juliet sat up, clutching the sheet to her chest. "How long?"

"I don't know."

Her mouth trembled, but no tears fell. Perhaps she had spent too many already. Perhaps pride had returned enough to stand guard.

Romeo sat up behind her. He wanted to touch her and did not trust whether touch would comfort or wound.

"I came because if I left without seeing you, then every story told about me would become the only story you had."

Juliet's voice shook.

"And I came because I needed you to judge me with your own eyes," he said. "Not your mother's words. Not my father's refusal to speak. Not Tybalt's death. Yours."

She turned back then. Her expression was raw enough to be worse than anger.

"And what if I had judged you guilty?"

"I am guilty."

"No." Her hand came to his face, rough with emotion now, forcing him to look at her. "Not like that. Do not hand me a simple answer because you think punishment is easier than being loved."

The words struck him with force enough that he had to close his eyes. When he opened them, she was closer.

"I loved Tybalt," she whispered. "Not cleanly. Not safely. Not always kindly. But I did. And he killed your friend."

"Mercutio stepped in because of me."

"Mercutio stepped in because he loved you."

Romeo found it hard to accept that Mercutio had died for love, but hearing it from Juliet, he knew in his heart it was true.

Juliet's thumb moved once along his cheekbone. "And you killed Tybalt because grief took you somewhere I hope never to see. I hate it. I hate that it happened. I hate that I understand more than I want to."

He lowered his eyes. She caught his chin and lifted it back.

"But I do not hate you."

Quiet closed around that. Then he pulled her into his arms. Juliet came willingly, fiercely, the sheet slipping between them, both of them bare and warm and already losing the night. They held each other not as lovers beginning now, but as people trying to memorize pressure, breath, skin, the exact measure of a body that would soon be absent. Another bird called.

Juliet made a small, furious sound against his neck. "I despise that bird."

Romeo's laugh was low and broken. "It may not be personal."

"It is extremely personal."

He held her tighter. For a while they stayed that way. When the first faint gray touched the edge of the curtains, Juliet pulled back and kissed him. Not carefully. Not sleepily. With the full knowledge of departure in it. The kiss carried the night, the bed, the canal stairs, the deaths, the names, the brutal road between them. Romeo answered until the kiss became reckless again, until his hand slid into her hair and hers pressed firmly against his bare chest, until both of them remembered too clearly how little time remained. He stopped first. Barely. Juliet's eyes opened.

"Do not be noble," she whispered.

"I'm trying to leave before I become stupid."

"I preferred you stupid."

"No, you didn't."

"For several hours, I did."

He smiled despite everything. It hurt. Then the smile faded.

"I need word from you," he said. "Anything. Through Galina. Through Father Lawrence. Through anyone they trust."

"I'll send it."

"Do not take risks you don't have to."

Her laugh was almost soundless. "That advice comes late from a man who climbed out of a rectory window."

"Fair."

She took his hand and pressed it to her mouth. "I will leave soon myself."

He stilled.

"What?"

"My mother will not let this remain mourning. She will turn it into a plan. Paris will become safer to them because you are a threat to them. Tybalt's death will become a reason to move me, marry me, bury me in whatever life looks most practical from my father's study."

The words were too precise to dismiss.

Romeo's fingers tightened around hers. "Come with me."

She closed her eyes. The fantasy held the whole room. A car. A road west. No Kapulet house. No Montague expectation. No Paris. No dawn dividing them into obedience and exile. Just distance and the two of them inside it. Then she opened her eyes.

"If I vanish with you now, they turn the whole city over before noon. Father Lawrence. Galina. Benvolio. Anyone who helped. Anyone who might have helped. I become the proof they need to make the war reality."

He knew it. That did not make hearing it easier.

"So what do you do?" he asked.

"I survive the day," she said. "I make them believe mourning has made me manageable. I listen. I learn where they intend to send me before they send me there. And I get word to you before they close the road."

He searched her face. "Juliet."

"I am not waiting to be rescued," she said.

"I know."

"No. Know it properly." She leaned closer. "If there is a road to you, I will find it. If there is not, I will make one."

The first thin light touched her face then. Dawn had found her. Romeo glanced toward the curtains. Outside, Washington was beginning to become itself again. Engines. Brakes. A distant door slamming. Ordinary life, indecent in its persistence. He rose from the bed. Juliet watched him dress.

There was something more intimate in that than she expected. The body she had held all night disappearing piece by piece into cloth. His shirt. His trousers. The priest's black coat. His wounded hand moving too slowly through the sleeve. The bruise at his ribs vanishing beneath fabric. The man becoming fugitive again. She stood and wrapped the sheet around herself. He paused with his hand on the coat.

"Don't," she said.

"What?"

"Look at me like goodbye has already won."

He came back to her at once. The kiss at the door was different from the others: tender enough to wound, desperate enough to remember the bed, and brief enough to let him leave. Juliet pressed something into his hand. He lowered his eyes.

A small hotel matchbook from the nightstand, the cover red and cream, the hotel title printed in cheap gold. On the inside flap, she had written with the pen from the desk: Alive. Yours. Find me. He closed his fingers around it.

"Juliet."

"Go."

He stayed where he was.

"Go," she said again, and this time her voice broke.

Romeo opened the door. The hallway outside was empty. He stepped through, then turned back once. Juliet stood in the dim room wrapped in a white sheet, hair loose, face pale in the first light, looking less like a girl he had loved too quickly and more like the woman he would not only die for but live for.

"I love you," he said.

Her expression changed—not surprise, but recognition.

"I love you too."

Then he left before dawn could take more. Juliet stood in the doorway until the elevator at the end of the hall opened, swallowed him, and closed. Only then did she shut the door.

Behind her, the room was warm, ruined, and full of him. The bed was tangled. His scent remained in the sheets. Rain had dried on the glass. The birds outside had become unashamed now, loud and ordinary and cruel. Juliet crossed to the window and pulled the curtain back. The canal below reflected the thin gray morning. The red sign had gone dark. She touched the glass once, then turned from it. There would be no sleeping now.

There would only be the house, Galina, her mother's eyes, her father's plans, Paris's patience, and somewhere west of the city, Romeo carrying a matchbook with her handwriting inside it. Juliet found her clothes on the floor and dressed quickly. Before she left, she smoothed the bed once, not to erase the night, but to honor it. Then she opened the door and stepped back into the life that thought it still owned her.

Chapter 20. Thursday Morning — Viktor's Study, Kapulet Townhouse, Georgetown

Viktor Kapulet did not like proposals made in mourning. Mourning made men reckless. It made women sentimental. It made families move too quickly and call panic protection. So when Paris Sokol stood in his study after Tybalt's death and asked, with perfect restraint, for Juliet's hand, Viktor's first instinct was refusal. Not forever. Only for now.

The study was closed against the gray morning. Rain tapped faintly against the windows. A fire burned low in the grate, more for ceremony than warmth. Ekaterina sat near the desk in black silk, her face pale but composed. Paris stood across from Viktor, hands folded behind his back, respectful enough to be proper and ambitious enough to be exactly what he was.

"You choose an ugly hour," Viktor said.

Paris inclined his head. "I know."

"Do you?"

"Yes." Paris's voice remained steady. "But ugly hours clarify what polite ones conceal. They show who has influence, who has courage, and who merely had good manners when nothing was at stake. I can take Juliet out of Washington tomorrow."

Ekaterina's eyes moved briefly to Viktor. He caught the look and disliked that he understood it.

Paris continued. "Juliet is exposed here. Tuesday night proved that. Tybalt's death proves more. The city is watching your house as if you and the Montagues are already at war, whether you believe it or not. Escalus is involved. Whatever privacy you still have is temporary."

"My daughter is not a commodity to be handed over lightly simply because the weather changed," Viktor said.

"No," Paris answered. "She is everything."

Viktor crossed to the window. Below, security had doubled at the front gate. Men moved in pairs now. No one laughed. No one smoked where he could see it. The townhouse had tightened around death and fear, and still Viktor could feel how many doors Washington had.

"Let me speak to my wife," Viktor said. "Please wait outside."

With a curt nod, Paris opened the door, stepped through it, and closed it behind him.

"She is grieving," Viktor said when he was sure Paris was out of earshot.

"She will grieve here or elsewhere," Ekaterina replied.

Ekaterina rose with measured care. "Do not look at me that way. I loved Tybalt. I loved all of our children, our nephews, and our nieces. She is the last."

"I know that."

"Then know this. Juliet is not safe here." Her voice cooled. "Paris offers distance from this house while you get your affairs straight, starting with this Romeo Montague. Paris offers legitimacy. A future not built entirely from our enemies' appetites, and away from crime. This is the future we wanted, the future we dreamed of for our children. For your legacy."

Viktor nodded. "She does not want him."

"She is young and does not know what she wants," Ekaterina said. "She is so shortsighted."

Viktor's expression hardened. "She is twenty-three."

"And still young enough to believe that she can bend the world to her feelings."

"She will hate us," he said flatly.

"Then that is the burden we will need to carry to ensure her safety and the security of your legacy," Ekaterina said.

A brief pause followed.

Then Viktor nodded. "Tell Paris to come back in."

Ekaterina opened the door and gave a quick wave. Paris returned. Once the door closed, Viktor smiled.

"What is your proposal?"

"Formal understanding first. Marriage later, when the timing can be made graceful." Paris paused. "But she should leave Washington tomorrow. Immediately. With me. Geneva first. Then wherever you decide is safest."

"Tomorrow," Viktor repeated.

"Yes."

He thought of Tybalt dead in the street. Juliet pale and defiant. Romeo Montague alive somewhere beyond reach. The dance at the masquerade. The way Tybalt had seen something in it and turned insult into violence.

Perhaps it was nothing. Perhaps it was only a dance. But a father did not need proof to know when danger had entered his house.

At last Viktor said, "Tomorrow morning."

Paris lowered his head once, a smile creasing his lips. Ekaterina closed her eyes for the briefest moment, not in relief exactly, but in confirmation.

Viktor turned back to them. "No announcement until she is out of the city. No public engagement yet. No spectacle."

"Of course," Paris said.

"You take her from Washington. Not as a husband. Not yet. As protection."

Paris accepted that with visible discipline. "Understood."

Viktor's gaze hardened. "And if she refuses?"

Ekaterina answered before Paris could.

"She won't be allowed to."

The fire shifted softly in the grate. Viktor did not correct her.

Chapter 21. Thursday Morning — Juliet's Rooms, Kapulet Townhouse, Georgetown

Juliet knew something had changed before her mother spoke. Ekaterina entered without knocking. That was not unusual. The absence of apology was ordinary in their house. But this time Galina came in behind her, and Galina's face had gone still in the careful way that meant her mother had brought bad news. Juliet stood near the window with Romeo's absence still on her skin.

She had slept only in fragments after returning from the hotel. The space still felt divided between who she had been before the canal stairs and who she had become after dawn. She had washed. Changed. Pinned her hair. Hidden every visible sign except the ones inside her body, where Romeo remained in her heart and her mind. Ekaterina looked her over.

"You will leave Washington tomorrow."

Juliet's hand tightened against the window frame. "What?"

"Tomorrow morning," Ekaterina said. "You will accompany Paris to Geneva."

At first, Juliet did not understand the words as a sentence. Then she did.

"No."

Ekaterina's face cooled. "Do not begin like this."

"No," Juliet said again. It was the only thing she could think of. Every fiber of her being screamed, *No.*

Galina's eyes flicked to her in warning.

Juliet could not take it. "I am not leaving with Paris."

"You are alive because this family understands protection better than you do," Ekaterina said. "You have been indulged, guarded, dressed, educated—"

"Owned," Juliet said.

The word cracked through the room.

Ekaterina's lips pressed thin. "Ungrateful girl."

Juliet laughed once. It came out too close to a sob. "Yes. Apparently wanting a life that belongs to me is ingratitude."

Her mother stepped closer. "You think defiance makes you profound? Tybalt is dead. The city is teetering on the verge of open warfare. Your father is doing what must be done."

"My father is selling me off."

Ekaterina's eyes flashed. "You think you are owed romance? A choice? Do you think I got one? Do you think Galina did? We play a role, and you are no longer a little girl. It is time for you to grow up. To marry. To become a mother. When you do, maybe then you will understand."

The door opened again, and her father, Viktor, came in. He had not dressed for the house. He wore his suit coat still, rain dark at one shoulder, his face cut into lines by grief and exhaustion. He looked first at Ekaterina, then Galina, then Juliet.

"What is this?" he asked.

"She refuses," Ekaterina said.

Viktor regarded his daughter. Juliet felt, absurdly, like a child again. Then she remembered Romeo's hand over hers in the hotel room. Romeo's voice before dawn. Juliet saying she would not be carried from one man's house to another and call it safety. She lifted her chin.

"I will not go with Paris."

Viktor's expression did not change at first. That was worse.

"You will," he said.

"No."

The strike came so fast Galina made a sound before Juliet did. Viktor's hand cracked across Juliet's face and turned her sideways. Her vision went white for one breath, then red at the edges. Her palm flew to her cheek. Heat spread under her skin, bright and humiliating. No one moved. Ekaterina's face had gone still.

Galina's hands had closed into fists at her sides, but she did not step forward. Not in front of them. Not yet. Only Juliet saw the fury in her eyes, carefully buried beneath the mask of service.

Viktor's voice dropped. "Do not mistake my mourning for weakness."

Juliet stared at him. The pain was not the worst of it. The worst was how quickly the room accepted the sound.

"You will leave tomorrow," Viktor said. "You will go where I send you. You will marry where I decide."

"I won't."

His eyes hardened. "Then you will have nothing. No family. No money. No protection. No Galina. No house. No father. I will disown you so completely this city will not remember you were ever mine."

Juliet's voice shook. Galina stepped in then, just enough.

"Sir," she said.

Viktor turned on her.

Galina lowered her eyes immediately, but her voice remained even. "Forgive me. Perhaps prayer would help. Confession. She is frightened and grieving. Father Lawrence may calm what we cannot."

Ekaterina's eyes narrowed. "You think a priest will make her obedient?"

"I think a priest may make her think," Galina said.

Juliet heard the difference. So did Ekaterina, perhaps, but not enough. Viktor turned to Juliet. She was crying now despite herself, tears hot over the cheek he had struck. He seemed to see them and not see them at once.

"One hour," he said.

Ekaterina drew a breath. "Viktor—"

"One hour," he repeated. "Galina takes her. Two guards. No calls. No stops. She returns here and prepares to leave."

Galina bowed her head. "Yes, sir."

Juliet stayed quiet. Viktor turned to the door. At the threshold, he stopped without looking back.

"If you shame this family again, Juliet, do not expect me to remember love before duty."

Then he left. Ekaterina lingered a moment longer. The anger in her face had thinned into something colder than regret.

"You could have made this easier," she said.

Juliet touched her burning cheek. "For whom?"

Ekaterina had no answer she wanted to give. She followed Viktor out and shut the door behind her. The room seemed frozen. Then Juliet broke. She sank onto the edge of the bed, one hand over her mouth, sobs coming hard enough to bend her forward. Galina crossed to her at once, not with the glass of medicine this time, not with instruction, but with both hands on Juliet's shoulders.

"My girl," she said softly.

Juliet shook her head. "He hit me."

"Yes."

"He hit me."

"I know."

The words were useless. They were also all Galina had.

Juliet looked up, tears running freely now. "He would really do it."

"Yes."

"Disown me."

"Yes."

"Take you from me."

Galina's lips tightened. "He would try."

Galina knelt in front of her, old bones and all, bringing their faces level. "Listen to me. You are at a crossroads. On one side is Paris. He offers much in material comfort, but I am afraid your soul will be crushed and that you will fade away. If you go with Romeo—"

Juliet glanced at her, tears still in her eyes.

Galina smiled. "Yes, child, I know that you were with him last night. But I also know he is flame. He burns so bright, with so much passion. But his passion will burn not only himself but you as well. You will live with him, but I am afraid you may not live a long life."

"I knew a man like that once. Even now, I long for him, and I know that he longs to be with me. But we have both made peace with the safe and secure road we took. I could not have children, but when we met, you became so much to me. You became my world. Your mother is right about children. They change your perspective, and for a while, they become your everything. A life preserver in an ocean of misery masquerading as safety and security."

Juliet stared at her. This was the most she had ever heard of Galina's past. The words should have sounded unreal. Instead, they sounded like a door being unlocked somewhere far inside the house.

"I love him."

Galina's face softened, not with surprise, but with the pain of having known too early where this would lead.

"Yes," she said, knowing that Juliet had already made her decision at this fork in the road.

"And they are sending me away tomorrow."

"Then we have very little time."

Juliet wiped at her face. "What do we do?"

"We go to confession," Galina said. "We speak to Father Lawrence. And this time, we do not ask him for comfort."

"What do we ask for?"

"A plan." Galina stood. "He is a remarkable man, but don't tell him I said that. He already has a big head."

Galina crossed to the wardrobe and pulled out Juliet's dark coat with quick, efficient movements. The preparations became practical under her hands. Gloves. Scarf. Handbag. Rosary. All the props of obedience arranged for revolt.

"I'll tell the guards you are washing your face," Galina said. "Then I'll call for the car."

Juliet nodded, though she felt hollowed out. Galina paused at the door and glanced back. Then she left, and the room fell quiet. Juliet sat on the edge of the bed, tears drying on her face, the heat of her father's strike still burning across one cheek. Her breath came unevenly. The townhouse moved beyond the door as if nothing had happened, as if daughters were struck and moved and married every day and the walls had long ago learned not to keep count.

Her gaze drifted to the writing desk, where the cream envelope lay half-hidden beneath a book. Rosaline's letter. Juliet had carried it from the masquerade into the night and then into the days that followed, always meaning to open it, always finding the world too violent, too crowded. Now the wax seal looked strangely bright in the gray room.

Rosaline had written before she died, before the attack, before Paris became Juliet's future, before Juliet had understood how quickly a girl's life could be moved by men claiming honor, love, and safety.

Juliet crossed to the desk and lifted the envelope. The lettering sat on the front in Rosaline's hand, stirring a painful mixture of memories: Rosaline herself, the friendship Juliet had lost, and Romeo holding her while the letter first came into her hands. For a moment, she only held it, gathering the strength to open whatever Rosaline had left behind. Then, with final resolve, she broke the seal. She slipped the paper from the envelope. It unfolded with a soft, delicate sound that felt out of place in the room.

Juliet read the first line, then the next. Her hand moved once to her mouth, but she kept reading. At first, shock crossed her face, then confusion, and finally something colder than either. Her eyes moved faster. Once, she stopped and went back, reading the same passage again as if the words might rearrange themselves into something kinder if she gave them another chance. They did not.

By the time she reached the final paragraph, the heat of her father's strike had vanished beneath a colder shock. Juliet lowered the letter and remained still for several seconds.

Beyond the door, the townhouse stayed quiet. Somewhere down the hall, a guard spoke softly into a radio. A car passed on the street below. Ordinary sounds. Unbearable sounds. Juliet looked at the letter again, then at the door where Galina had gone, then back to the words Rosaline had left behind.

"Paris Sokol," she whispered.

The words left her mouth with disgust, rage, and fear—or something colder than all three: an awakening. The letter trembled in her hand. Whatever she had thought she was going to ask Father Lawrence for, it was not enough anymore.

Chapter 22. Thursday Afternoon — St. Ignatius Parish, Georgetown

The guards stayed outside the church because Galina made it sound as though listening to confession would embarrass Ekaterina more than it would protect Juliet. That was enough. Men like that feared two things: failure, and women with authority reporting failure upward.

Juliet entered St. Ignatius with her cheek still burning from her father's hand and Rosaline's letter hidden inside her coat. The church was nearly empty. Candles lit near the side chapel. Rain tapped lightly against the stained glass. Father Lawrence stood near the sacristy door, and the moment he saw her face, something in him stilled. Galina gave one small shake of her head: not here. Father Lawrence understood at once and led them to the east confessional.

Juliet entered the left stall. Galina took the right. Father Lawrence sat between them, enclosed by old wood, shadow, and the thin screen that made hidden things easier to say. For a moment, none of them spoke. The church seemed to listen with them, old stone holding its breath while the rain whispered against the glass.

Then Father Lawrence asked, "Who struck you?"

Juliet shut her eyes.

Galina answered for her. "Viktor."

The priest's breath changed, only slightly, but Juliet heard it. So did Galina. Father Lawrence did not curse, did not raise his voice, did not make the mistake of wasting anger where action was needed.

After a moment, he said, "Tell me what has happened."

Juliet reached into her coat and slid Rosaline's letter beneath the screen. "Read it."

Father Lawrence took the pages. The paper shifted softly in his hands, and Juliet listened to him unfold it. At first, the silence that followed was ordinary reading silence. Then it sharpened.

He turned a page, stopped, and went back. On the other side of the booth, Galina sat perfectly still. She had already read the letter in Juliet's room, her face growing colder with each line, but hearing Father Lawrence discover the truth made the fear feel new again.

Father Lawrence read to the end without speaking. Then he read part of it again. When he finally folded the letter, his voice had changed.

"Who else has seen this?"

"Only the three of us," Juliet said.

"Keep it that way."

"You believe her?"

"I believe Rosaline wrote this because she feared something and had no safer way to say it." He passed the letter back beneath the screen. "And I believe Paris Sokol's timing is more than inconvenient."

Juliet held the pages tightly in her lap. "Then you understand why I cannot go with him."

"Yes."

"Can you help me leave?"

Father Lawrence did not answer quickly enough, and that frightened her more than a refusal would have.

Galina said softly, "Lawrence."

"I can help," he said at last. "But not cleanly."

Juliet's fingers tightened over the letter. Inside the center compartment, Father Lawrence opened a small drawer. Glass clicked against wood. When his hand appeared beneath the screen, he held a small vial wrapped in linen.

Juliet stared at it. "What is that?"

"A door," he said. "Badly disguised as death."

The church seemed colder. Galina stayed motionless. "You kept it."

"I kept many things I hoped never to use."

Juliet could barely take her eyes from the vial. "What does it do?"

"It slows the body. Pulse, heat, and breathing. Not forever. Long enough to be mistaken."

"Mistaken for dead," Juliet said.

"Yes."

The word entered the confessional and stayed there.

Father Lawrence leaned closer to the screen. "Your family will not want a hospital. Not after Tybalt. Not after the attack. Not with Paris waiting and the city watching. They will want privacy because privacy gives them control. They will call the family doctor and keep the police away as long as they can."

"The family doctor," Galina said.

"Yes."

Juliet turned toward the shadow of him through the grille. "You know him?"

"I know his failings." Father Lawrence's voice went dry. "He diagnoses the room before the patient. He fears Viktor. He dislikes outside records. And if your mother means to force you onto a plane in the morning, she will likely ask him to give you something tonight so you sleep and behave."

Galina understood first. "A sedative."

"A sedative," Father Lawrence said. "If he leaves medicine in the room, that becomes the story. Not because it is true, but because it is convenient. A grieving daughter. A full bottle the night before. An empty bottle in the morning. A letter beside it. He will see the bottle before he sees you."

Juliet's mouth went dry. "You want them to believe I took his medicine."

"I want them to believe what they are already prepared to believe," Father Lawrence said. "If the bottle is nearly empty and a letter is waiting, the doctor will not search for miracles. He will look for a pulse, fail to find one, and let fear finish the diagnosis."

Galina's voice remained low. "And if he does not leave medicine?"

"Then we do not use that part of the story. The plan changes. But if he does, do not waste the opportunity."

Juliet looked down at the vial wrapped in linen. "And after?"

"If it works, Paris cannot take you to Geneva. He will arrive for a living bride and find a dead one. Your parents will be too shocked to question the first explanation placed in front of them. They will move you privately, most likely to the family chapel or another place they control, because mourning in that house will still be treated as a family matter."

"And Romeo?"

"I will send Brother John tonight. We cannot chance the Feds monitoring his email or phone calls. Ellis, his father's retainer, will meet him soon at the safe house. Romeo must know before he hears any other version."

Juliet closed her eyes once. Romeo was somewhere beyond the city, believing or not believing whatever reached him first. The thought of him hearing that she was dead, even falsely, made her feel as if the plan had already hurt him.

"He will come if he thinks I'm dead," she said.

"Yes," Father Lawrence answered, "he is ruled by his passions. That is his greatest strength, and his greatest weakness."

Juliet stared at the vial. It was smaller than she expected, which made it worse.

"If there is another road," Father Lawrence said, "we take it. If your father relents, if Paris withdraws, if the house gives you even one real opening, we do not use this."

"They won't," Juliet said.

"Let me finish pretending they might."

Galina's voice softened. "Juliet."

Juliet thought of Geneva. Paris. Her father's hand. Her mother calling obedience gratitude. Rosaline's letter trembling open under her fingers. Romeo leaving before dawn with exile waiting for him. Everything narrowed until the vial no longer looked like death. It looked like the only door still unlocked. She reached for it. Father Lawrence did not release it immediately.

"Not for romance," he said. "Not for drama. Not because dying looks easier than living."

Juliet met the shadow of his eyes through the screen.

"No," she said. "Because I am alive, and I intend to stay that way. Paris will not take me away."

Only then did he let go. Juliet wrapped the vial back in linen and hid it beside Rosaline's letter. A knock struck the outer wood almost at once.

One of the guards. "Miss Kapulet?"

Father Lawrence raised his voice. "Confession is not improved by interruption."

The guard retreated.

Galina stood first, her face already returning to the careful mask she wore in the Kapulet house. "We go back," she said. "You look frightened and exhausted. That will be useful."

"I am frightened and exhausted."

"Good," Galina said. "Use the truth when it serves. Paris Sokol may think he understands what he has done. He does not. Understanding and regret will come for him."

Chapter 23. Thursday Late Afternoon — Juliet's Rooms, Kapulet Townhouse, Georgetown

By the time Juliet returned from St. Ignatius, obedience had become theater. She let the guards help her from the car. She let Galina keep a hand at her elbow. She walked through the side entrance with her head slightly lowered, not in surrender, but because women in her family knew the value of letting men mistake exhaustion for defeat.

Her father's mark still burned across her cheek. Rosaline's letter and Father Lawrence's vial lay hidden in her handbag, pressed side by side like two irreconcilable futures. Ekaterina waited in the upstairs hall with the house doctor beside her. Juliet stopped when she saw him.

He was an anxious little man in a tailored coat, his medical bag held too tightly in one hand. He had been useful to the family for years because he understood what was expected of him before anyone had to say it aloud. He treated bruises without questions, and bullet and knife wounds without records.

Ekaterina looked first at Juliet's face, then at Galina. "Well?"

Juliet made herself answer quietly. "I'm tired."

That was true. Truth, Galina had said, was useful when it served.

Ekaterina's expression softened by a fraction. "Then perhaps confession did some good."

"Perhaps."

The doctor stepped forward, studying Juliet with cautious concern. "You look pale, Miss Kapulet."

"I have had a difficult few days," Juliet said.

"Yes, of course." He glanced at Ekaterina before continuing. "Your mother asked me to remain tonight. Only as a precaution. You are expected to travel in the morning, and after the shock you have suffered, it would be unwise to let you pass the night without observation."

Juliet looked at her mother. "Observation?"

"Do not be dramatic," Ekaterina said. "He will not sit at your bedside like a jailer. But he will remain in the house."

"In case I become inconvenient?"

"In case you become hysterical," Ekaterina said, and her voice sharpened. "Your departure is set for morning. Six o'clock. You will sleep tonight."

The doctor opened his bag and removed the amber bottle. "The same medicine as before. It should help you rest."

Juliet looked at the bottle. Galina did too.

The doctor held it up briefly, as if the fullness of the bottle itself proved his caution. "One dose only. No more. It is mild, but after emotional distress, even mild medicine should be treated with respect."

He set it on the small tray near the bedroom door beside a clean glass and a folded linen napkin. The bottle was full enough that the liquid line caught the light.

Ekaterina accepted that with a nod. "Galina will see that she takes it."

"Yes, madam," Galina said.

Juliet stayed quiet. Inside her room, the preparations for Geneva had already begun. A dark travel dress hung from the wardrobe door. Gloves lay beside a folded scarf. A case sat open near the bed, half-filled with clothes Juliet had not chosen. Paris was not in the room. Still, he was everywhere. Galina shut the door and locked it. At first, neither woman moved. Then Juliet took the cream envelope from her handbag.

Juliet held it tightly. "I keep thinking I misread it."

"You did not."

Juliet looked down at Rosaline's handwriting, then forced herself to hand the letter over.

Galina accepted it carefully and folded it once. "I will keep this with me. If your room is searched, or your handbag is taken, this cannot be found."

Juliet nodded, though giving it up made her feel strangely exposed. Then her gaze drifted to the bedside table. The amber bottle from the house doctor sat there beside the glass of water, exactly where he had left it, still full enough to condemn her once it was not.

"The doctor's medicine?" Juliet asked.

"Yes." Galina picked up the bottle, read the label, and stood for a moment with it in her hand. "This is what he will remember."

She moved to the bathroom and poured most of it into the sink. The sound was small and ordinary, which made it worse. When she returned, only a little liquid moved at the bottom of the bottle.

Galina set it back beside the glass where it could be easily seen. "But you will not drink it. It is only here for the story they need to believe."

Juliet nodded, then reached into her handbag and drew out a second envelope, this one addressed to her parents. She set it beside the doctor's medicine with careful hands.

Galina's face tightened. "Juliet."

"They will believe I meant to die," Juliet said.

For a moment, Galina did not answer. Then she looked from the envelope to the amber bottle and forced herself not to flinch.

"Yes," she said. "They will."

Juliet reached into her handbag again and took out Father Lawrence's vial. It looked smaller in her room than it had in the confessional. Smaller, and therefore worse.

Galina's face did not change, but her voice lowered. "Are you certain?"

"No."

"Good. Certainty makes people stupid."

Juliet turned toward the travel dress. Geneva waited in dark wool and careful buttons. Paris waited somewhere beyond the house, probably already informed of her surrender to him, and the thought made her skin crawl. She thought of Romeo west of the city, not knowing. She thought of Rosaline's letter. She thought of her father's hand.

"No," Juliet said at last. "I'm not certain. But I am certain that if I leave with Paris, my life is over."

Galina nodded once, as if that was the only certainty that mattered. The townhouse settled around them. A guard moved somewhere in the hallway. Downstairs, a door closed softly. Juliet imagined her mother in the study, arranging grief into travel plans; her father speaking in low tones over the phone; Paris waiting for morning as if morning belonged to him.

Juliet uncorked Father Lawrence's vial. Her hand shook. Galina saw her courage faltering and took the vial from her. She reached for the glass on the bedside table, poured the contents into it, and handed it back. The liquid vanished without color.

Juliet stared at the glass. "It looks like nothing."

"The worst things usually do."

Juliet lifted it, then stopped. "What if Romeo doesn't get the message?"

"He will."

"You don't know that."

"No," Galina said. "I don't."

Juliet turned to the door. Then the window. Then the bed where she had slept as a girl, a prisoner, a daughter, and now something else entirely. She drank.

The water was cool and ordinary. At first, nothing happened. Then fear did. Not pain, not yet, only the body's first recognition that a door had closed behind her and another had not opened yet. Juliet swayed.

Galina caught her before she could drop the glass. "Bed."

Juliet obeyed. Her legs felt too distant by the time she reached the mattress. Galina eased her down, drew the blanket over her, and arranged her hands as if she had simply fallen asleep.

Then Galina crossed back to the bedside table and made sure everything was prepared: the doctor's bottle, nearly empty now; the glass; the envelope addressed to Juliet's parents. The room told the story it needed to tell.

Galina turned out the light and moved to the door. For a moment, she looked back at Juliet lying pale and still beneath the blanket.

"Sleep, Juliet," Galina whispered. "Soon, you will be free."

Then she left the room.

Chapter 24. Friday Pre-dawn — Juliet's Rooms, Kapulet Townhouse, Georgetown

Paris arrived before six, while the townhouse was still half-dark and already preparing to move. Lights burned in the lower hall. A black SUV idled against the curb outside, its exhaust ghosting in the cold morning air, and one of Viktor's men stood near the front window with a phone pressed to his ear.

He entered through the side door with his coat buttoned, his gloves in one hand, and the clean, composed look of a man arriving to collect what had been promised to him. Ekaterina met him in the hall dressed as though she were traveling too, though she was not going anywhere. Her hair was pinned, her pearls were fastened, and her face had been arranged with the same care as the rooms downstairs.

"Paris," she said.

He kissed her cheek. "Madam."

Viktor stood near the foot of the staircase, watching him. Paris turned at once and offered the proper greeting, and Viktor answered with a brief nod toward the door.

"The car is ready."

"So is the plane," Paris said. "Dulles has been handled. Geneva is expecting us."

Ekaterina looked toward the stairs. "She should be dressed by now."

Galina appeared from the service corridor with Juliet's smaller case in both hands. She had tied her apron over a dark dress, and she kept her eyes lowered as she crossed the hall, moving with the quiet efficiency expected of her.

"I will wake her," Galina said.

Ekaterina turned. "No. Take that to the car. Then see that the blue case is brought down from my room. I will get Juliet."

Galina stopped for only the length of one breath. "Yes, madam."

Ekaterina gathered her skirt and went up the stairs, leaving the three of them below with the soft mechanical sound of the waiting car beyond the door. Paris watched her disappear at the landing before turning back to Viktor.

"Was the night quiet?" Paris asked.

"Quiet enough."

"She understands?"

Viktor looked toward the front door, where the pale edge of morning had begun to press against the glass. "She will do as she is told."

Paris lowered his gloves into one hand and smoothed them once with his thumb. "Once we are in Geneva, there will be fewer distractions."

Viktor did not answer. Galina had reached the door by then, but her fingers remained wrapped around the handle of Juliet's case even after one of the guards reached to take it from her. Then Ekaterina screamed.

The sound came from above them, keen enough to cut through every locked room in the house. Galina dropped the case. Viktor was already moving, taking the stairs two at a time, and Paris followed close behind him, one hand catching the banister as he turned the landing too quickly. Galina came after them, her shoes striking the wood without rhythm.

Juliet's bedroom door stood open. Ekaterina was on the bed, bent over her daughter with one hand beneath Juliet's shoulder and the other against her face, trying to pull warmth or breath or answer from a body that gave her nothing back.

"Juliet," she said. "Juliet."

The blanket had slipped to Juliet's waist. Her blonde hair lay loose against the pillow, and one hand rested open beside her, palm turned upward, fingers slightly curled. Ekaterina shook her once, then again, harder the second time, calling for her as if volume could drag her back from wherever she had gone.

Viktor crossed the room and caught his wife under the arms. She fought him, her nails dragging once against the coverlet as he pulled her back from the bed.

"She's cold," Ekaterina screamed. "Viktor, she's cold."

"Get the doctor," Viktor said.

A guard vanished from the doorway. Paris had stopped just inside the room, his gaze moving from Juliet's face to the bedside table, where the amber bottle stood beside the water glass. Beside it lay the cream envelope addressed to Viktor and Ekaterina Kapulet.

Galina stopped at the foot of the bed. She did not touch Juliet. She did not touch the table. She only folded both hands in front of her and lowered her head.

The doctor came in with his bag half-open and his coat pulled over a shirt not yet properly buttoned. He saw Juliet first, then Ekaterina struggling in Viktor's grip, then the bottle on the table.

"Move back," he said.

No one moved.

He looked at Viktor. "Move back."

Viktor dragged Ekaterina another step from the mattress. She bent forward in his arms as though the bed still had hold of her, one hand reaching uselessly toward Juliet while the doctor moved in beside the pillow.

He took Juliet's wrist. The room held still while he shifted his fingers against her skin, searching. Then he reached for her throat and pressed two fingers beneath her jaw. His own breathing had become loud in the hush. He took the stethoscope from his bag, put the earpieces in with trembling hands, and set the disc against Juliet's chest. He listened, moved it, and listened again. Ekaterina's mouth opened, but no sound came out. The doctor lifted his head and looked at the bottle. His face changed before he reached for it.

"This was full last night," he said.

No one responded. He picked it up, read the label anyway, and turned it once in his hand. Only a little liquid moved at the bottom. When he set it down again, the glass gave a soft, terrible click against the table.

"She has overdosed," he said. "The sleeping medicine. She took almost all of it."

Paris reached for the envelope. Galina's eyes lifted as he opened it, but she remained where she stood. The paper trembled in his hands as he read the first lines. He did not finish quickly. He stood beside Juliet's bed and read the rest without speaking, holding the letter with both hands as though it had become too heavy for one.

The doctor bent over Juliet again. He checked her wrist, her throat, and her chest, but nothing changed. At last, he straightened and turned toward Viktor and Galina. His eyes lowered before he shook his head. "I am sorry."

Paris turned toward Viktor and held out the letter. Viktor did not take it at first. Ekaterina twisted in his arms, reaching for the bed again.

"My baby," she said, the words tearing loose from somewhere beneath speech.

Viktor released one arm from around his wife and took the letter. Ekaterina slipped from his hold and fell to her knees beside the bed, gathering Juliet's hand against her mouth. Her body folded over the side of the mattress, pearls hanging loose from her throat, her pinned hair coming apart one black strand at a time. Viktor read. The paper shook once. Only once.

Galina's head bowed lower. Paris stepped back until his shoulder touched the wall. Viktor remained where he stood, the letter crushed slightly in one hand, his eyes fixed on the bed, while Ekaterina pressed Juliet's cold hand harder against her mouth.

Outside, the waiting car kept running.

Chapter 25. Friday Morning — Western Maryland

Romeo had not slept. The safe house stood at the edge of a tree line west of the city, far enough from Washington that the air smelled different and close enough that exile still felt like cowardice. It was an old parish property tucked beyond a narrow gravel road, white clapboard and peeling shutters, with a frozen garden behind it and mountains rising dark beyond the field. Brother John had left him there before dawn with two instructions. Stay inside. Wait for Father Lawrence. Romeo had done neither well.

He stood by the kitchen window, staring at the gray morning with Juliet's hotel matchbook in one hand and her sapphire earring in the other. The cheap red-and-cream cover had softened from being opened too many times. Inside, her handwriting waited like proof that the night had happened. Alive. Yours. Find me. He had read it until the words stopped feeling like language and became a wound. The knock came just after eight. Romeo turned so quickly the chair beside him scraped the floor. For a wild instant, he thought it might be Father Lawrence. A message. A correction. Some road back.

Then Ellis, a loyal Montague man his father had sent to help protect him, stepped inside. Romeo knew before the old man spoke that something was off. It was in his eyes, the way he held himself.

"What's wrong?" Romeo asked.

Ellis closed the door. Rain clung to his shoulders. He looked older than Romeo had ever seen him. Older than the driver who had carried him through childhood. Older than the retainer who had stood half a step behind Salvatore Montague through courtrooms, funerals, and deals that required discretion more than loyalty.

"Tell me," Romeo said.

Ellis did not take off his gloves. "Juliet Kapulet was found in her room before dawn."

The kitchen went very quiet. Romeo gripped the edge of the table.

"No."

"The family doctor was called. No ambulance. No hospital. No outside confirmation."

"No."

"They are keeping it private."

"Stop."

Ellis swallowed once. "She was pronounced dead."

The words did not enter Romeo all at once. They struck and scattered. Found in her room. Family doctor. No hospital. Pronounced dead. Dead. The matchbook fell from his hand.

Romeo bent as if he meant to pick it up, but his knees failed before his fingers reached the floor. He caught himself against the table, an exhale tearing through him in one sound too raw to be speech.

Ellis stepped forward. "Sir—"

"Don't."

The old man stopped. Romeo stared at the matchbook on the floor. Alive. Yours. Find me. A sound came out of him then, not loud, but ruined. He pressed one hand to his mouth as if he could keep the grief inside by force. It did not work. It moved through him anyway, tearing open every place already broken. Rosaline first.

The truck lights. Glass. Blood in black hair. The cream envelope at her feet. His hands shaking against wrecked metal while strangers ran toward a car already past saving. Then Mercutio. His friend's mouth bright with blood. You killed me. The anger and love in his eyes, both alive until they were not. Then Tybalt. The brick. The awful small sound. Juliet's cousin gone slack beneath him while rage left Romeo too late to matter. And now Juliet. Juliet who had stood under the red sign. Juliet who had touched his wounds. Juliet who had written Alive and then vanished into death before morning could finish taking him from her. Romeo laughed once.

It was a terrible sound.

"I'm cursed," he said.

Ellis's face tightened. "No."

"Yes." Romeo lifted his eyes. They were dry now. That was worse. "Every woman I love dies. Every friend who stands too close to me dies. Every man I hate becomes more blood on my hands. What would you call that?"

"Grief."

Romeo shook his head.

"No. Grief is what happens after loss. But I leave a wake of death everywhere I go."

Ellis stepped closer. "Father Lawrence may have word."

"Where is it?"

"He has not sent."

"Then he has nothing."

"You don't know that."

Romeo turned to him, and Ellis went silent. There was nothing useful left in the room. No priest. No message. No law. No Juliet alive in hiding. Only a private death inside a Kapulet house and the city already preparing to swallow the truth before it reached daylight.

"Where is she?" Romeo asked.

"The townhouse, for now. They have not moved her yet. Kapulet wants privacy."

Romeo stood.

Ellis understood the movement immediately. "No."

"I'm going back."

"You cannot."

"I am."

"If you enter D.C., you die before you reach the door."

"Then I die closer to her."

Ellis grabbed his arm. "Listen to yourself."

Romeo glanced at the old man's hand. Ellis released him slowly.

"Romeo."

But Romeo had already left the room. He took Father Lawrence's black coat from the chair, Juliet's sapphire earring, and the matchbook from the floor. He put the earring and matchbook in his pocket, then walked out into the rain. He did not take the car.

At first, he did not know where he was going. Only away from the house. Away from the waiting. Away from Brother John's careful instructions and Father Lawrence's absent message. He walked down the gravel road until it met asphalt, then along the shoulder toward the small town below the ridge. Trucks hissed past on wet pavement. Cold rain found his collar and slid beneath it. He barely felt it. The town was waking badly.

Gas station lights. A laundromat. A pharmacy not yet open. A man smoking beneath the awning of a closed bar. Two boys arguing near a bus stop. A woman unlocking a café door with her hood pulled low. Romeo passed all of it like a man moving through someone else's country. Then he saw the dealer.

Not because the man looked dramatic. He looked ordinary, except to a man who had spent his whole life in the company of Montague men. He recognized the subtle clues. Gray hoodie. Damp cap. A cigarette cupped in one hand. He stood near the alley beside the bar, speaking low to a man with shaking fingers. Romeo stopped. The dealer looked over. Something in Romeo's face made him straighten.

"You need something?"

Romeo heard himself answer before the part of him still capable of caution could intervene.

"Something strong."

The dealer glanced at his coat, his bruised face, his city shoes dark with rain and mud. "You look like you need a hospital."

"I need sleep."

The man's expression changed by a fraction. "What kind?" the dealer asked.

Romeo held his gaze.

"The kind a man does not wake from."

The dealer looked away first. "Bad idea," he said. "I don't need that kind of heat."

A faint smile touched Romeo's mouth. "No. You need money."

The dealer's eyes came back to him then, edged with insult and need. Romeo reached into his coat and pulled out a folded stack of bills, enough to make the morning around them change. Enough to buy discretion. Enough to buy what no man should sell. Neither of them moved. Rain ticked in the gutter. A bottle rolled somewhere under a dumpster. The alley smelled of stale beer, wet concrete, and ruined choices. The dealer looked at the money, then away from it, and that was how Romeo knew he would take it.

"You don't know me," the man said.

"No," Romeo answered. "But I know hunger when I see it."

The dealer's mouth tightened. Pride fought need and lost by inches. His coat was too thin for the weather, one shoe had split at the side, and his fingers were red from cold when they flexed.

"This is poison money," the dealer said.

"All money is, eventually."

Romeo held the cash out. The dealer stared at it a moment longer.

"Costs extra."

Romeo's voice was flat. "Then take extra."

The exchange was brief and ugly, small enough to disappear into the morning: a fold of paper, a warning Romeo did not listen to, and a hand closing around something no larger than mercy and far less kind. He tucked it inside Father Lawrence's coat, then turned toward the road back east.

Ellis found him twenty minutes later near the edge of town. The sedan pulled alongside him slowly, and the window lowered. The old man glanced at Romeo once, then at the road ahead.

"Get in."

Romeo kept walking.

"Get in," Ellis said again. "If you mean to go back to Washington, at least allow me the dignity of failing to stop you properly."

Romeo stopped. Then he opened the passenger door and got in. The car pulled away. Fields blurred past, then highway, then signs for the District. Romeo sat very still with Juliet's sapphire earring in one pocket and the paper fold in the other, both hidden like rival sacraments: one for love, one for sleep.

He would see her once more. He would touch her face. Tell her he had come. Tell her he had not stayed away. Tell her that if the world had taken every living road, then he would follow the only one left. He was done being separated from the dead. Washington rose ahead, gray and wet under the low sky. Romeo closed his eyes. By the time he opened them again, he had decided everything.

Chapter 26. Friday Night — St. Ignatius Parish, Georgetown

Father Lawrence knew something had failed when Brother John returned with the note still in his hand. The priest stood in the rectory hall with his coat already on and the chapel keys in his palm. He had been ready to leave for the Kapulet house for nearly twenty minutes. Juliet would wake soon, if the timing held. She would wake cold, disoriented, and surrounded by a family grieving for her, and Father Lawrence needed to be there before that happened. Still, he had waited until the last possible moment.

He had waited because Romeo needed to know the truth before any rumor reached him. He had waited because a boy already carrying Rosaline, Mercutio, and Tybalt in his heart could not be left to hear that Juliet was dead and believe it. Now Brother John stood in the doorway, rain on his shoulders and the unopened envelope in his hand.

Father Lawrence reached for it before his mind allowed him to understand what it meant. "You found him?"

Brother John's face was pale. "No."

The word passed between them and made the old house feel suddenly too large.

"What do you mean, no?"

"He was gone from the safe house."

"When?"

"I don't know. Ellis was gone too. No one answered. The watcher at the road said a sedan left earlier, headed east."

"East."

Brother John stayed silent. Father Lawrence stared at the unopened message in his hand. Juliet lives. Come to St. Ignatius. All will be explained. The paper seemed obscene now, too late while still perfectly clear, a mercy that had failed by minutes. Romeo had not been told about the plan. He had no reason to doubt the story the city would give him: Juliet dead in her room, apparent suicide.

Father Lawrence closed his eyes against the pain he had helped unleash. "He'll go to her," he said.

Brother John nodded once. "Yes."

The priest opened his eyes, dread sharpening into action. "I've waited too long already. Stay here in case Romeo comes. I'm going to the Kapulet house before Juliet wakes."

"We still have time?" Brother John asked.

"Not much," Father Lawrence said.

Brother John's face tightened. Father Lawrence paused only long enough to look toward the church nave, where candles burned.

"God forgive me," he said under his breath.

Then he opened the rectory door and stepped into the rain. He had taken only three steps down from the rectory when two men in dark coats moved from beneath the church awning and blocked the path.

"Father Lawrence?" one of them asked.

Father Lawrence stopped, his face tightening. "Yes."

The man showed his credentials. "Federal Bureau of Investigation. We need you to come with us."

Father Lawrence looked at the badge, then past him in the direction of the Kapulet house. Rain gathered at the edge of his collar and slid cold beneath it.

"I am in the middle of a pastoral emergency."

"We understand, and we are aware of Miss Kapulet."

"No," Father Lawrence said. "You truly do not." He paused and looked at them. "On what grounds am I coming with you?"

The first agent kept his voice measured. "U.S. Attorney Escalus has questions regarding Romeo Montague, Juliet Kapulet, and your possible role in concealing material information connected to an active investigation."

Father Lawrence's hand closed around the failed note in his pocket. Juliet lives. Come to St. Ignatius. All will be explained. A note that had not reached the boy in time. A mercy that had failed by minutes.

"I do not have time for this," Father Lawrence said.

One of the agents shifted slightly, not threatening, but not moving either. "Father, this is not optional. The only choice is whether you wear handcuffs."

With that, the agents led a reluctant Father Lawrence to a waiting sedan. As the car pulled away, dread settled deep in his stomach.

Chapter 27. Saturday Pre-dawn — East Parlor, Kapulet Townhouse, Georgetown

The Kapulet house was quiet because grief had exhausted it.

The night had spent everyone badly. Lights burned in the wrong rooms. Guards stood at the front doors, the garden gate, and the main stair, watching the places a living enemy might try to enter. No one watched the old conservatory passage closely enough. No one expected a grieving man to come for the dead.

Romeo entered through that forgotten line of the house with rain on his coat and death in his pocket.

Ellis had gotten him as far as the service lane and no farther. The old man had gripped the steering wheel with both hands and said nothing for nearly a full minute before Romeo opened the car door.

Then, finally, he said, "If there is any reason left to come out, take it."

Romeo had not answered.

Now he moved through a corridor that smelled faintly of lilies, floor polish, and extinguished candles. The Kapulet house had changed since the masquerade. No music now. No servants carrying champagne. No laughter polished thin enough for senators and diplomats. Only lamps left burning, flowers arranged too early, and the heavy stillness of a house waiting to bury its daughter.

He should have been caught. He was not.

Security had tightened around the obvious places: the front entrance, the garden doors, the upstairs hall, the room where Juliet lay. But grief made even disciplined men predictable. They watched approaches. They watched doors. They watched the living. Romeo found the neglected seam between those concerns and moved through it.

At the far end of the passage, the east parlor doors stood separating Romeo from his love.

Inside, candlelight trembled over dark furniture and white flowers. Heavy curtains had been drawn. A low table had been cleared, and the chairs had been moved to make space for the narrow bier placed near the windows. The parlor had once been made for tea, conversation, and careful family arrangements. Now it held Juliet.

Romeo stepped inside the dim room, where faint streetlamp light peered through the curtains. The room was shadowed enough that he did not see Paris.

Paris Sokol stood in the shadow near the far curtain, one hand resting against the dark wood of the window frame, his face half-hidden by the fold of the drape. He had come quietly, before the house fully gathered itself, to see what had become of the future he had almost secured. When he heard movement, he did not speak. Then Romeo entered, and Paris stayed silent, because some instincts were older than pride, and what came through the door did not look like a rival arriving. It looked like a man already half-buried.

Romeo crossed the room slowly.

Juliet lay beneath a white coverlet, her blonde hair arranged over the pillow, her hands folded at her waist. Someone had dressed her in a black gown and fastened one small sapphire at her ear. Not both. One. The missing earring burned in Romeo's pocket. At first, he could not move. His world narrowed to her face: beautiful, still, terribly off. That was the word his mind found and would not release. Wrong.

Death should have changed her more. It should have made her strange. But Juliet looked like herself in a sleep too deep for ordinary waking. Her mouth was softer than death deserved. Her skin was pale, yes, too pale, but the line of her cheek remained the line he had touched under the red sign, in the hotel room, before dawn took him from her.

Romeo reached the bier and stopped, his hand hovering over her face. He was afraid to touch her, afraid she would be cold, and afraid she would not be. At last, he set two fingers against her cheek. Cool. Not ice. Not warmth. Something between. Something hope could make cruel use of if he let it.

He closed his eyes. "Juliet."

Calling her did nothing. He touched her hand next, then stared at her chest. It felt strange and terrible when he realized he was holding his own breath, waiting for hers, watching for the natural rise and fall of life.

Behind him, in the shadow, Paris watched. He saw Romeo's hand shake. He saw the way the Montague boy leaned over Juliet, not like a thief, not like a conqueror, but like someone approaching an altar he knew he had no right to touch and could not bear to leave.

Romeo took the hotel matchbook from his pocket and set it beside her folded hands. Red-and-cream cardboard. Cheap gold letters. Her handwriting hidden inside. Alive. Yours. Find me.

A bitter sound left him. "You told me to find you," he whispered. "And I did. I did."

His voice broke on the last word. He bent his head over her hand, and for a while, he only breathed. The grief did not arrive as sobbing. That would have been easier. It came as memory, one after another, each sharper than the last: Rosaline in the wreckage, black hair against broken glass; Mercutio coughing blood and still trying to make dying sound like something clever men could mock; Tybalt's face under him, surprised at the end; Juliet beneath the red sign; Juliet in his arms, warm and alive and choosing him in a world that had given her every reason not to. Every road behind him had a body on it.

Every love had become a grave.

"I am cursed," he said softly.

The word sounded too small in the parlor. Too small for the damage. Paris's hand tightened once against the curtain. Romeo reached into the inner pocket of Father Lawrence's black coat and closed his fingers around the paper fold he had bought in the rain. The easy road. The final road. The one no father, priest, court, or city could follow once he took it. He simply held the packet. His breathing slowed into something frighteningly calm, and he turned to Juliet again.

If she had truly gone where he could not reach her, then why should he remain among men who kept turning love into violence? What was left for him in a world that had taken Rosaline, Mercutio, and Juliet, then left him alive beside Tybalt's death like punishment disguised as life? He opened his hand. The packet lay against his palm. Small. Ugly. Nothing like mercy. Romeo stared at it.

Paris saw it, and understanding moved through him with a cold, precise shock. He almost stepped forward then, almost spoke—not to save Romeo, perhaps, not exactly, but because the act, once witnessed, would make him part of it. A man in shadow becomes responsible for the shape of what he allows. Before Paris could move, Romeo bent over Juliet and set the packet on the edge of the bier. Not taken. Not refused. Not yet.

His mouth touched her forehead, then her cheek, then, finally, her lips. The kiss was soft at first because she could not answer. Then it changed. Not into hunger, but into farewell, into every unsaid thing compressed into one ruined act of tenderness. Romeo kissed her as if apology could move through skin, as if exhale could be shared backward, as if love might wake whatever death had silenced if only he gave enough of himself to it. An old line came to him from some schoolroom, some play, some cruel inheritance of romance and ruin. Thus with a kiss— No. Romeo froze. His eyes opened. No.

The word did not come from reason. Reason had abandoned him hours ago. It came from her. From Juliet in the hotel room, telling him not to hand her a simple answer because punishment was easier than being loved while broken.

From Juliet at the canal stairs, saying she had tried to hate him and could not. From Juliet beneath the first gray light of morning, telling him she would find a road if one existed and make one if it did not.

If he took the easy road, he would make her love another body to bury. He would make Benvolio live with one more failure. He would give Mercutio's last anger the shape of truth. He would prove Father Lawrence right about young men and death accepting invitations. And Juliet—Juliet had not chosen him so he could abandon every hard thing and call it devotion. Romeo pulled back from her mouth. His hand closed around the packet. For a taut moment, Paris thought he would use it.

Instead, Romeo crushed it in his fist. Not enough to destroy it. Enough to choose against it. He set it on the floor beside him and pushed it away with the back of his hand.

"I can't," Romeo whispered.

His voice broke.

"I can't follow you there. Not like that."

The words came slowly, as if each one had to be dragged over broken glass.

"I want to. God help me, I want to. But if there is any part of you left in this world, any part that loved me, then it deserves better than my cowardice dressed as romance."

His voice shook.

"I don't know how to live without you."

He pressed his forehead to hers.

"But I will. If that is what loving you costs, I will."

Paris stared from the shadows.

Romeo took Juliet's hand between both of his. His bandaged palm brushed her folded fingers, and he bowed over her like a penitent. Then Juliet's fingers moved. So slightly that at first he thought grief had invented it. Romeo froze and lowered his eyes. Nothing. Then again, a faint twitch against his hand.

His breath stopped. "Juliet?"

No answer. He leaned closer, searching her face so intently the rest of the room vanished. Her lips parted, and a thin breath entered her. Small. Fragile. Real. Romeo staggered back half a step, then caught himself on the edge of the bier.

"No."

This time the word was not denial. It was wonder. Juliet's lashes trembled. Her mouth moved again, searching for breath. The drug loosened its hold like darkness thinning reluctantly before dawn. Her body jerked once, not violently, but with the painful confusion of returning to itself from somewhere too far away.

Romeo caught her shoulders. “Juliet. Juliet, look at me.”

Her eyes opened. They were unfocused at first, dark and terrified, seeing ceiling, candlelight, white flowers, then his face. For a suspended instant, she did not understand. Then she did.

“Romeo?”

The word came out as almost no sound at all. He laughed once, broken and disbelieving, then gathered her into his arms. Juliet clung to him with a strength that did not match the pallor of her face. Her hands gripped his coat, his hair, the back of his neck. She was cold and weak and shaking so hard he had to hold her up, but she was alive. Alive against him. Alive beneath his hands. Alive enough to gasp when he kissed her.

The kiss was chaos. Relief, terror, pain, fury, love—all of it colliding too quickly for either of them to separate. Romeo kissed her mouth, her face, her hair, then her mouth again. Juliet answered as if waking itself required him, as if every exhale had to be pulled through the contact between them. Her fingers twisted in his coat. A sob broke from her, then from him. Neither cared who heard.

“You’re alive,” he said against her mouth.

“So are you.”

“I thought—”

“I know.”

“I came to—”

“I know.” Her hand found his face, clumsy and desperate. “I know.”

He shut his eyes at the touch. Paris stepped out of the shadow. The movement was small, but the parlor heard it anyway. Romeo turned first, still holding Juliet against him. Juliet followed his gaze. Paris stood near the curtain, pale, composed, and watching them with a look that held shock, calculation, and something almost like injury. A brief pause followed.

Then Paris said quietly, “So it is true.”

Chapter 28. Saturday Pre-dawn — East Parlor, Kapulet Townhouse, Georgetown

Paris stood near the heavy curtain, composed by habit rather than control. His hand stayed steady, but the rest of him had begun to betray him: a pulse jumped at his jaw, his smile kept missing its shape, and whenever his gaze slid from Juliet's living face to Romeo's arms around her, something in him cracked wider.

Streetlight spilled low through the dark room, holding all three of them among the flowers and the death that had not quite happened. Juliet's voice came thin from the drug and waking.

"Paris?"

His smile appeared and vanished. "You were supposed to be safe." He swallowed. "Not dead. Safe. Mine—" He stopped, hearing the word too late, and tried to smooth it away. "Safe. I meant safe."

Romeo shifted in front of Juliet, protective by instinct. Paris noticed the movement, and his jaw set as if Romeo had touched something that belonged to him.

"Careful," Paris said. The word was meant for Romeo, but his eyes stayed on Juliet. "I am not a stupid man, and you have already made me adjust too many plans these last few days."

His hand slipped inside his coat. Romeo's expression went blank, and Juliet's hand closed around his sleeve.

"Don't."

Paris drew the gun slowly, not with panic, but with the strange ceremony of a man who had rehearsed several endings and disliked the one unfolding in front of him. The small black weapon looked obscene against the polished cut of his coat.

"You see?" Paris said softly. "That is the difference between us. Romeo moves because he feels. I prepare because I think." His mouth twitched. "I prepare, and still people ruin things."

The last sentence came out too fast. Paris seemed to hear the crack in it. He smiled harder, and the smile made the crack worse.

Romeo stood still, his eyes on the weapon, while Juliet's fingers tightened on his sleeve. Paris's gaze moved to those fingers, and there it was again—not pain, not even anger at first, but insult so intimate it felt indecent, as if Juliet's hand on Romeo were a private theft.

"You watched us," Juliet said.

Paris laughed once. It was too short and too bright. "I watched many things. Your house. Your guards. Your father's habits. Your mother's fears. Tybalt's temper." His eyes cut to Romeo. "And him, once he became a problem."

"A problem," Romeo said.

"A disruption," Paris snapped, then pressed his lips together as if the correction had cost him more than the insult. "An intrusion into a design I had been refining for years."

Juliet drew herself upright on the bier. Her body was weak, but her voice found a sharper place. "My life was your design?"

"Your life was never going to be yours alone." Paris stepped closer, gun still low but ready. "Not with your name. Not with your father's reach. Not with what your mother understood you could become." His gaze moved over her face with a devotion so warped it looked like illness. "You were born into consequence, Juliet. I was the only man honest enough to plan for it."

Juliet's face hardened. "You sent the men that night."

Paris opened his mouth, closed it, and gave a small nod that looked almost like relief. The confession had found its door, and now he could not seem to shut it.

"The attack served several purposes," he said.

Juliet went cold. Even the last heaviness of the drug seemed to vanish beneath the horror of what he had admitted.

Paris continued, quicker now, as if speed could make murder sound like strategy. "Your father needed urgency. Tybalt needed a target. And you—you needed a reason to leave with me."

"They grabbed her," Romeo said. "They hurt her."

Paris's expression flickered. "They were not supposed to harm her. That part was unfortunate. Your mother was quite upset."

"That is your defense?"

"That is the truth," Paris said flatly.

Juliet stared at him from the bier, pale and trembling. "You talk about me as if I belonged to you. As if I had no choice."

Paris's polished mask split. Not entirely. Just enough for the thing beneath it to breathe.

"You were supposed to." He drew the words out as if they should have been obvious to everyone. "That was the understanding."

Juliet's lips parted. "What understanding?"

"Your mother's." Paris's voice lowered, turning almost tender in a way that made the room colder. "Not in writing. Not formally. She was too clever for that. But she made it clear enough. She knew what I could offer. She knew what I wanted. She knew you would be safer with a man who understood how to keep what was his."

"What was his," Juliet repeated.

Paris heard himself again and smiled tightly, as if the words had betrayed him but not enough to shame him. "Do not pretend to be naïve. Families like yours do not leave futures to chance. Your mother understood that before your father did. She understood your value."

"My value."

"Yes," he said, too quickly. "Your value. Your name. Your blood. Your position. Your beauty. The doors you open by simply standing in front of them." His voice frayed. "You think that is ownership because you have been taught to despise order. I call it stewardship."

"No," Juliet said. "You manipulated me and my family."

His eyes flashed. "Because I loved you."

"That is not love."

For one second, Paris looked genuinely wounded. Then the wound turned mean. "Do you think I began wanting you at the masquerade? I knew years ago. I knew your schools, your drivers, your tutors. I knew which rooms you avoided and which windows you used when you wanted the house to forget you."

Romeo moved half a step forward, but Juliet's hand tightened on his sleeve.

"Wait," she whispered.

Paris noticed the touch, and his mouth twitched with dislike.

"You misunderstand me if you think this is common obsession," he said. "This is love. Not the crude kind. Not the desperate kind." His hand tightened around the gun. "One day, away from this house and this boy and all their noise, you will understand. Come to Geneva with me."

Juliet's hand tightened on Romeo's sleeve, and she forced herself fully upright. The movement cost her. The last of Father Lawrence's drug still clung to her limbs, but she slid one foot carefully to the floor, then the other, using the edge of the bier to steady herself until she stood close behind Romeo.

Juliet's eyes hardened. "Rosaline warned me about you."

Paris went still.

His composure truly slipped. Not much. Only a tightening near the eyes, a small failure of the mouth. But Juliet saw it, and Romeo did too.

"So the letter reached you," Paris said.

"Yes."

Something ugly moved through his expression, too quick to be called anger and too intimate to be called surprise. "Even in death she haunts me."

Romeo's body changed beside her. "You knew about the letter."

Paris looked at him then, and the confession fed itself now, not as a neat explanation, but as a leak he could not stop.

"Rosaline worked for me then," Paris said.

Romeo went very still. Paris saw the wound open and leaned toward it.

Paris returned his attention to Juliet, but his smile kept finding Romeo. "Rosaline knew you. Your moods. Your friendships. What frightened you. What bored you. What made you soften. She gave me small things and never understood how useful they were."

"You used her," Juliet whispered.

"She was useful until she was not."

The room seemed to recoil from the sentence. Paris heard it, heard himself, and flushed with irritation rather than shame.

Romeo's voice came low. "What did Rosaline find?"

Paris turned to him, and whatever restraint he had left became cruelty. "The photographs. The files. Notes. Names. Routes. Drivers. Juliet's file." His mouth curved. "That surprised her."

Romeo's hands curled once at his sides.

"Rosaline came to me," Paris continued. "Angry. Disgusted. Suddenly moral. She said I had used her. She said I was sick. She said she would tell Juliet everything."

Juliet's voice broke. "So you killed her."

Paris's face hardened, but his eyes had gone bright, almost feverish.

"She forced the matter."

The words were quiet. Too quiet. Then he seemed to need them larger, crueler, irreversible.

"The accident was clean," he said. "A delivery truck. A wet road. Rosaline beside you. No murder. Just the young, rash Montague heir tangled in a hit-and-run."

Romeo's expression emptied. Whatever fragile purpose had kept him from taking the powder and following Juliet into the dark seemed to recede under the force of Rosaline's memory. She saw only the change in him: the way his face went still, the way his grief seemed to lose its shape and become something more dangerous. Paris saw it too, and his smile came back worse than before.

That smile broke something in Romeo. His body shifted, but Paris's gun was already leveled against him.

"Do not," Paris said.

The parlor went tense. Juliet stood close behind Romeo, one hand locked around his sleeve, the other braced against the edge of the bier to keep herself upright. Her eyes moved from the gun to Romeo and back again. Then the door handle turned.

Ekaterina's voice came from the hall, edged with suspicion. "Paris, why are the lights off?"

Paris's eyes flicked toward the door as Ekaterina's hand emerged through the doorway and found the switch.

Light flooded the room.

Romeo closed the distance in one brutal movement and drove into Paris before the gun could come back cleanly. He caught him by the front of his shirt and slammed him backward into the wall with enough force to rattle the picture frame beside his shoulder. Paris's head struck plaster, and his smile vanished. The gun jerked off line.

Romeo struck him once, and the sound cracked through the room. Paris's finger tightened on the trigger, and a shot tore into the upper molding near the curtain. Plaster burst; the small CCTV lens above it flashed once and went dark. The door flew open.

Ekaterina stood in the doorway. For a frozen instant, her eyes took in the unbelievable: Juliet alive beside the bier, Romeo Montague in the room, Paris bleeding, and the gun lying on the floor between them.

"Juliet?" Ekaterina cried out, her voice breaking through the room.

Paris dropped hard to one knee, blood bright at his mouth. The gun slipped from his hand and skidded across the floor, coming to rest near Ekaterina's feet.

Romeo hauled Paris upright and threw him across the side table. White lilies spilled from the vase as it shattered, scattering across the rug like bones.

Juliet moved from beside the bier, still unsteady. "Romeo!"

Romeo did not hear her. There was no grace, no staged exchange of clever words. There was only anguish finding the man who had murdered Rosaline, stalked Juliet, and set fire to both houses. Paris had dressed obsession as love and called ruin devotion. Now Romeo's anguish, his anger, his rage, had a target.

"Romeo!" Juliet exclaimed.

He did not stop. Romeo drove Paris to the floor. Paris desperately reached for the gun, but it was just outside his grasp. Ekaterina saw the weapon, then crossed the last step and snatched it from the floor before either man could reach it.

Romeo caught Paris by the throat and began choking him. Paris's eyes widened, the lunatic certainty finally breaking into the fear that he was about to die.

"You killed Rosaline," Romeo screamed.

Paris clawed at his wrist.

"You hurt Juliet!" Romeo's grip tightened. "You sent men into her house!"

Paris's face reddened. Juliet reached Romeo, weak and trembling but fierce enough to break through the killing haze in his eyes. She caught his face in both hands.

"Romeo. Look at me." She spoke with urgent, calm sweetness, like a woman desperately trying to reach him.

Romeo did not respond. She pressed closer, forcing herself between his rage and its target.

"Look at me," she commanded and begged at once.

Romeo's breathing shook. Paris rasped beneath him. Slowly, painfully, Romeo's eyes found hers.

Juliet held him there. "Not this. Not again."

"He killed her," Romeo said, voice broken.

"I know."

"He killed Rosaline."

"I know."

"He deserves it."

"Yes," Juliet whispered. "He does."

Juliet's thumbs moved over his cheekbones. "But you do not deserve to become this for him. I have seen you. You are a better man."

Romeo's grip loosened by a fraction.

"He took Rosaline," she said. "He tried to take me. Do not give him the rest of you too."

For a terrible instant, Romeo stayed where he was. Then he released Paris and shoved himself backward, breathing hard, staring down at the man on the floor as if Paris were a cliff he had almost stepped over.

Paris coughed and rolled onto his side among shattered lilies and glass as Romeo stood slowly. Romeo's fists clenched. Then, one finger at a time, he opened his hands. Juliet saw it, and so did Ekaterina. Romeo turned from Paris, broken and gasping on the rug, to Juliet.

"I won't," he said, voice rough. "Not again."

Juliet's expression changed, not with relief alone, but with recognition. He had reached the same fire and chosen not to burn. Romeo stepped away from Paris. That was the victory. That was the change.

Then Ekaterina lifted the gun she had taken from the floor.

"Montague." The word came from her mouth like poison.

Romeo turned, and the shot cracked through the parlor. He jerked backward, the bullet catching him high in the side. Juliet screamed as he staggered, one hand flying to the wound, and struck the edge of the bier so violently he nearly fell. Blood spread beneath his fingers.

"No!" Juliet rushed to him, catching him before he went down completely. "Romeo!"

He was breathing. Wounded, but breathing.

Ekaterina kept the gun raised, her face white with hatred. "Montague," she said again, softer now, as if the word itself explained everything. "Always Montague."

Paris stirred on the floor. "Ekaterina," he rasped.

Her eyes snapped to him.

Paris tried to lift one bloody hand. "We had—"

The second shot ended him. Paris fell back against the rug, eyes open, mouth still shaped around whatever words he was about to say. Juliet froze. Romeo's weight sagged against her.

Then the door behind Ekaterina burst open wider, and Viktor entered first, with Galina at his shoulder and two Kapulet men behind them.

Chapter 29. Saturday Dawn — East Parlor, Kapulet Townhouse, Georgetown

For a stunned instant, everyone froze. Under full light, the parlor had become a nightmare: Juliet alive beside the bier arranged for her death; Romeo Montague bleeding in her arms; Paris Sokol dead on the rug among shattered lilies and glass; Ekaterina standing between them all with the gun still in her hand.

Viktor saw Juliet first, and his expression changed. Not with understanding. Not yet. With the stunned, helpless shock of a father seeing his dead daughter breathe.

"Juliet?"

The word left him raw. Behind him, Galina made a small, broken sound before covering her mouth with both hands.

Juliet tightened her arms around Romeo. "He's hurt."

That seemed to wake the room. Romeo's hand was pressed high against his side, blood spreading beneath his fingers. His breathing was shallow and uneven, but he was breathing.

Galina moved first. "Hold him."

Juliet already was. Galina crossed the room quickly, ignoring Paris's body, ignoring Ekaterina, ignoring the gun until one of Viktor's men stepped toward it. Viktor lifted one hand, stopping him.

"Katya," Viktor said.

Ekaterina turned toward him slowly. Her face was white, but her eyes still burned. The gun hung at her side now, smoke faint at the barrel.

"He was here," she said. "The Montague was here with her."

Viktor's gaze moved from Romeo to Paris, who lay on his back, his eyes and mouth open, blood darkening the front of his shirt. Then Viktor turned to Ekaterina.

"You shot Paris."

"He had betrayed us."

The answer came too quickly. Too cleanly.

Juliet lifted her head. "He confessed."

Ekaterina's eyes cut to her. "You are drugged and confused."

"No." Juliet's voice trembled, but it did not break. "He confessed. He sent the men to the masquerade. He arranged the attack. He killed Rosaline."

Viktor went still. Galina, kneeling now beside Romeo, looked up sharply, and Ekaterina's hand tightened around the gun.

"He was lying," Ekaterina said.

Romeo dragged in a broken inhale. "No."

The word cost him. Juliet looked down at him. "Don't speak."

Romeo's eyes stayed on Viktor. "Paris said it."

Viktor's face hardened by degrees, grief giving way to something colder. "Katya," he said again, but this time her name sounded like a question he already feared the answer to.

Ekaterina's lips pressed tight. "You are listening to a Montague."

The word came from her with the same hatred as before, but now it sounded less like certainty and more like defense. Galina rose slowly and reached into her coat, withdrawing the folded cream envelope.

Rosaline's letter.

Ekaterina saw it, and her gaze narrowed in keen focus. Viktor saw her reaction.

Galina held the letter out to him. "Read it."

Ekaterina's voice sharpened. "Don't."

Viktor's gaze moved to his wife. For the first time Juliet could remember, Ekaterina looked afraid of what he might learn. Viktor took the letter. Everyone seemed to wait while he read. At first his face did not change. Then the page shifted slightly in his hand. His eyes went back over one line, then another. He read to the end, then lowered the letter slowly. The grief in him altered. Not vanished. Altered.

"Paris," he said, and the word came out like something rotten finally exposed to light.

Ekaterina's lips parted. "Viktor—"

"You knew."

"I knew he was useful."

"You knew enough."

"I knew he could move her out of danger."

"You knew enough," Viktor repeated.

The words struck harder the second time.

Ekaterina's face broke open, not into softness, but fury. "And what should I have done? Wait for another child to die while you coddled her? While you let her play at freedom with a Montague?" Her eyes burned as they moved to Romeo. "That family has brought ruin into this house. Montague. Always Montague. Your wars. Your softness. Your hesitation. Tybalt is dead. Our family is gone piece by piece, and you still could not make one hard choice for the daughter we had left."

Galina helped Romeo higher, enough that he could stand with Juliet's support, though barely. He swayed as soon as his weight shifted, and Juliet tightened one arm around him until he steadied.

Juliet stepped forward. Romeo tried to stop her, his fingers catching weakly at her wrist, but she gently pulled free.

"No," she said.

Ekaterina regarded her as if she had forgotten Juliet could speak. Juliet stood between her mother and the wounded man behind her, between the dead man on the rug and the father holding Rosaline's letter.

"No," Juliet said again.

Ekaterina's eyes flashed. "Everything I did was to protect you."

"You protected an idea of me," Juliet said. "A daughter who would do whatever you wanted. A daughter who could be traded to guarantee your legacy, not my father's."

"That is not true."

"It is." Juliet's voice shook, but did not break. "You knew Paris wanted me with a sick obsession, and you fed him. You used him, just like you wanted to use me."

Ekaterina lifted the gun again, not quite aiming. Not yet. Galina's whole body went tense.

Viktor said calmly, "Katya."

Ekaterina ignored him. "And what is he?" she demanded, pointing toward Romeo with the weapon. "What is Romeo Montague? A savior? A lover? A boy with blood on both hands and a name that has already cost this house too much?"

Romeo's breathing hitched. Blood darkened his side. Still, he lifted his head and met her eyes. Ekaterina's hatred did not flinch. Juliet turned slightly, enough to see him, enough to see the wound. Then she faced her parents again.

"Romeo did not choose my life for me," she said. "He gave me the choice everyone else kept trying to take away."

"Choice," Ekaterina spat. "The word children use when they cannot see consequence."

"No," Juliet said. "It is the word adults fear when control begins to fail."

The parlor went silent. Viktor regarded his daughter. Not the girl he had dressed in silk and locked behind guards. Not the heir to his legacy he thought he could spirit away into a fairy-tale marriage. Not the child he had struck and expected obedience from afterward. A woman. Hurt, furious, and alive.

Juliet's voice lowered. "You no longer get to decide what is best for me. Neither of you. Not with a ring. Not with a ticket. Not with money. Not with threats. Not even with love."

Ekaterina inhaled sharply. Viktor offered no reply.

Juliet faced him now, and the words cost more. "You hit me."

His expression changed. Only slightly. Enough.

"You told me I would have nothing if I refused you," she said. "So hear me plainly. I would rather have nothing that belongs to me than everything that requires me to vanish."

Galina's eyes shone, but she stayed where she was. Romeo swayed behind Juliet, and that motion broke something practical in the room.

Galina spoke up. "He is bleeding."

Viktor's gaze shifted to Romeo, and the two men regarded each other across the ruined parlor. Romeo was pale, bleeding, barely upright, but he did not look away. Not from Viktor. Not from the man who had struck Juliet, threatened her, tried to send her away, and now held the letter proving the future he had chosen was poison.

"Enough," Viktor said.

Ekaterina turned toward him. "Viktor—"

"I said enough."

The parlor stilled under the weight of his voice. Ekaterina stared at him as if he had betrayed her. Perhaps he had. Or perhaps he had finally stopped.

Viktor held out his hand. "Give me the gun."

"No."

"Katya."

The word came quietly. Not tenderly. Not harshly. Finally. Ekaterina looked from him to Juliet, then to Romeo, then to Paris dead among the lilies. Something in her face crumpled and hardened again almost in the same exhale. She placed the gun in Viktor's hand as if surrendering a war she intended to remember. Viktor passed it to one of his men without looking away from his wife. Then he turned to Galina.

"Take them."

Ekaterina recoiled. "You cannot—"

"Take them," Viktor repeated.

Galina did not ask if he was sure. She did not waste miracles by questioning them. She slipped one arm around Romeo's back, and Juliet moved under his other shoulder, supporting him with all the strength she had left. Romeo hissed through his teeth as the wound pulled.

Viktor looked to one of the guards. “The side service hall. No cameras. No one stops them.”

The guard stared. “Sir?”

Viktor’s voice turned lethal. “Did I stutter?”

“No, sir.”

Juliet started toward the door, half-carrying Romeo with Galina’s help. At the threshold, Romeo stopped, not because he could afford to, but because some things demanded witness.

He looked first at Ekaterina. Her eyes were all rage and hatred, grief turned outward because inward would have destroyed her. To her, he would always be Montague first, man second, and perhaps never anything else. Romeo absorbed that. Then he turned to Viktor.

Viktor regarded him wordlessly. No forgiveness there. No welcome. No blessing for the violence between them. Only assessment. Romeo had seen men appraise enemies before, but this was different. Harder to read. A father measuring the man his daughter had chosen against the ruin around him, against the blood on his hands. Viktor’s eyes dropped once to Romeo’s wound, then returned to his face.

A single nod.

Romeo returned the smallest nod he could manage. Then Juliet pulled him through the door.

Behind them, Ekaterina made a sound too broken to be a word. Viktor did not follow.

Galina led Juliet and Romeo down the side hall, past servants frozen against the wall, past the closed doors of a house that had tried to bury its daughter and found her walking out alive. At the service entrance, rain waited over Georgetown. Juliet tightened her grip on Romeo. He leaned into her. Together, they stepped out of the Kapulet house.

Chapter 30. Saturday Afternoon — Federal Conference Room, Washington, D.C.

Benvolio had been taken out of the interview room before he understood why. No one explained it, not at first. A deputy opened the gray door, two agents stepped in, and one of them said, "U.S. Attorney Escalus wants you upstairs."

Benvolio looked down at his hands. They were clean now, but he could still see Mercutio's blood in the lines of his skin.

"Am I being charged?" he asked.

The agent did not answer, which was not comforting.

They took him to a conference room with no recorder on the table. That was the first thing Benvolio noticed. The second was Escalus standing near the far window, still in his coat, his face drawn and colorless with mourning for Mercutio, his cousin, held too tightly beneath the demands of office.

Salvatore Montague sat at one end of the table with Ellis behind him. The old man's silence was controlled, but not calm. His eyes moved once to the door when Benvolio entered, then past him, searching for the person who had not come in behind him.

Romeo.

Only when Salvatore did not find him did his face close again. Father Lawrence sat near the middle of the table, and when Benvolio entered, the priest offered him the faintest smile, more sorrow than greeting.

Then the door opened again, and Viktor Kapulet entered with his lawyer beside him. The lawyer carried a cream envelope sealed in clear evidence plastic and a black drive.

Salvatore rose slowly. "Where is my son?"

Viktor stopped just inside the room. For a moment, neither man looked like a patriarch. They looked like fathers who had both run out of places to put their fear.

"Alive," Viktor said. "Wounded, but alive."

Salvatore's composure broke for the briefest instant. It was gone almost as soon as it appeared, but Benvolio saw it. So did Ellis, whose hand tightened against the back of Salvatore's chair.

A charged hush held the room until Escalus said, "Sit down. Both of you."

It was not a request. Salvatore and Ellis sat. Viktor and his lawyer did the same. Benvolio remained standing until Escalus glanced at him.

"You as well, Agent Omerti."

Benvolio sat.

Viktor's lawyer placed the envelope and the drive on the table. Viktor rested one hand near them but did not touch either.

"Juliet Kapulet and Romeo Montague are alive," he said, his voice sounding older than it had any right to sound. "Paris Sokol is not. He was responsible for the attack on my house."

Salvatore's eyes sharpened. "Responsible how?"

Viktor looked toward the envelope. "This was found in my house. The letter belonged to Rosaline. The recording is from the east parlor."

"Recording?" Salvatore asked.

"A CCTV camera above the curtain line," Viktor said. "Old. Angled. I used that room for doorways and glimpses, not for conversations. It caught more than I expected, and then the first shot killed the feed."

Escalus picked up the envelope first and read the name on the front: Juliet Kapulet. Then he broke the seal on the plastic sleeve, withdrew the folded pages, and began to read. His expression changed before his voice did, and when he spoke, the room stilled.

"Juliet," Escalus read, "I do not know how to begin except with the part I should have said years ago. I am sorry. I am sorry for whatever stupid, proud, childish thing I let become silence between us. The truth is, I do not even understand the fight anymore. I only know I stayed away too long, and that has weighed on me more than I ever admitted."

Benvolio closed his eyes briefly. Rosaline. Even dead, she sounded alive.

Escalus continued. "I was hired to consult for Paris Shipping. That was the official title. Consultant. It sounded important enough to make my mother proud and vague enough to mean almost anything. Most of the work was courier work: legal papers, private contracts, sealed documents moving between lawyers, government offices, and clients who preferred not to use ordinary channels. Apparently, I had good manners, a respectable name, and a talent for getting into rooms. Who would have thought?"

Escalus read on. "At first I thought Paris was only ambitious. Polished. Cold. The usual Washington disease with better tailoring. But he kept asking questions about you. Casual questions, at first. Too casual. Where you spent your time. Who you spent it with. Whether Galina was always with you. Whether you still danced. Whether you still liked galleries. I told myself he was making conversation, but then I started to notice the pattern."

Salvatore's gaze moved once to Viktor. Viktor did not look away from the letter.

"One afternoon I was waiting in his study. He had taken a call and left me there too long. I was bored, and yes, nosy. I think I was born a little nosy, and for once, that may have been a virtue. I saw a file on his desk marked with your name. Juliet Kapulet. I opened it."

Escalus paused briefly. "When I say there were photographs, I do not mean a few. I mean years of them. And they were not public photographs. They were taken from odd angles and at strange times. You at charity events. Outside venues. In London. In Vienna. In Georgetown. School functions. Galleries. Restaurants. Your father's terrace. You laughing. Reading. Waiting for cars. Walking with Galina. He had notes, dates, routes, names of drivers, names of guards."

Viktor lowered his eyes, and Escalus's voice hardened.

"I confronted him. I told him it was sick. I told him I was quitting. I told him you would know. He did not deny it. He confessed he was in love with you, and he simply wanted to know more. Juliet, listen to me: Paris is dangerous. Do not trust him.

"And there is something else. He had access to private information he should not have had. There is a leak inside your house. Be careful who you tell. Some of those photographs were taken from inside your home."

A hush moved through the conference room. Escalus read the last lines more quietly.

"I should have come back before this. I should have said I was sorry when there was still time for us to laugh about whatever broke us. I am sorry I let pride become years. I am sorry I made apology more difficult than it needed to be.

"Do not trust Paris. Do not be alone with him. And please, if there is still any piece of the girl who was once my friend left for me, forgive me."

Escalus lowered the letter, and for a moment no one answered.

Then Viktor pushed the black drive toward him. "The video."

Escalus signaled one of the agents by the wall. The agent took the drive, connected it to the room monitor, and stepped back. The screen lit, and the east parlor appeared from a high, colorless angle: Juliet on the bier, Romeo between her and Paris, Paris emerging from the curtain shadow. The audio was thin but clear enough.

"You were supposed to be safe," Paris said from the screen. "Not dead. Safe. Mine—" His recorded voice faltered. "Safe. I meant safe."

Benvolio felt the room tighten. On the monitor, Paris drew the gun and began speaking faster, his aristocratic polish slipping away by degrees.

"I watched many things," Paris said. "Your house. Your guards. Your father's habits. Your mother's fears. Tybalt's temper. And him, once he became a problem."

The video continued. Paris called Romeo a disruption, then spoke of purpose, families, money, borders, futures, and men who understood power. His voice kept trying to regain its former smoothness and failing.

"The attack served several purposes," Paris said. "Your father needed urgency. Tybalt needed a target. And you—you needed a reason to leave with me."

The conference room went cold.

On the screen, Juliet accused him of treating her like property. Paris stepped closer, and the camera caught his face from above: no longer handsome, no longer composed, only feverishly certain and visibly unraveling.

"You were supposed to," he said. "You were promised to me. I waited."

Escalus did not pause the recording. No one asked him to.

"Do you think I began wanting you at the masquerade?" Paris said. "I knew years ago."

The recording moved on to Rosaline: her employment, the photographs, the files, the notes, names, routes, and drivers. Paris's confession came out in pieces at first, then too quickly, as if exposure had become a kind of appetite.

"She forced the matter," Paris said.

Salvatore's face tightened. Then Paris's voice continued from the screen.

"The accident was clean. A delivery truck. A wet road. Rosaline beside you. No murder. Just the Montague heir tangled in a hit-and-run."

A low sound came from Salvatore. Not anger, not quite. Something older and more personal. Benvolio looked down at his hands.

On the monitor, Ekaterina's hand appeared at the door. Her voice cut through the room: "Paris, why are the lights off?" Light flooded the parlor. Romeo crossed the frame and drove Paris into the wall. A shot cracked, and the bullet tore into the upper molding near the camera. The image flashed once, then broke into black.

For an instant, the audio remained: Juliet's scream, a crash, Ekaterina crying her daughter's name. Then that died too, and the monitor showed nothing.

Salvatore turned to Viktor. "Convenient."

Viktor's face did not change. "It does not erase what came before it."

"And Paris?" Salvatore asked. "What happened to him?"

"Killed by my security personnel," Viktor said.

Salvatore gave a humorless smile. "Very convenient. Though I will admit, I liked Rosaline very much. Had I known what he had done to her, I might have wanted to be present."

Viktor raised his head. For one strange moment, the two men regarded each other not as enemies, but as fathers standing among ruins neither of them had built alone.

Escalus turned off the monitor and faced both families. "Paris Sokol engineered the attack on the Kapulet house. He arranged the crash that killed Rosaline. He manipulated both families toward retaliation. He used Tybalt's temper, Kapulet fear, Montague pride, and Washington discretion. The principal architect of this violence is dead."

Viktor offered no reply. Salvatore's eyes remained on the blank monitor.

Escalus continued, colder now. "As to Romeo Montague, this office is not blind to what happened in the street. Tybalt Kapulet brought a knife into a public fight, stabbed Mercutio Vale, and continued an armed confrontation during active gunfire with a Federal agent. Romeo's response was violent. It was also part of the same chain of force Paris deliberately set in motion."

Salvatore looked up sharply.

Escalus held his gaze, then Viktor's. "Could a prosecutor try to make a case out of that death? Perhaps. Could your lawyers spend the next year turning self-defense, imperfect defense, provocation, heat of passion, and retaliation into a public battlefield? Certainly. And while they did, every man loyal to either house would hear only one thing: the law had chosen a side."

No one spoke.

"That is what Paris wanted," Escalus said. "He wanted this city to turn procedure into permission. He wanted grief converted into warrants, indictments, retaliation, and blood. I will not let the law finish what he started."

Benvolio exhaled before he realized he had been holding it in.

Escalus looked at him briefly, then back to the fathers. "This office will not pursue charges against Romeo Montague for Tybalt Kapulet's death. Based on the complete sequence, the armed circumstances, and the evidence that Paris Sokol provoked these events to ignite violence between the houses, Romeo's actions will be treated within the framework of self-defense and prosecutorial discretion."

Viktor's expression did not soften, but he accepted the words without protest.

Escalus's voice lowered. "That does not make the dead less dead. It does not make Romeo clean. It does not make Tybalt innocent. It means the law will not be used as the next knife."

No one argued.

Escalus stepped closer to the table. "There will be no war in this city. Not today. Not under the cover of mourning. Not under the excuse of honor. Not between Montague and Kapulet."

Salvatore's expression hardened. Viktor's face remained unreadable.

Escalus looked between them. "Peace is no longer sentiment. It is survival."

The conference room fell silent. Then Salvatore turned to Viktor. "Where are they?" Benvolio knew what he meant. Romeo. Juliet. Viktor answered him. "I don't know." Salvatore studied him for a long moment. A heavy pause settled between the two fathers and all their dead.

Then Viktor said, quieter, "For now, let them be free. Let them live their lives without us."

Salvatore held his gaze. His answer came not as agreement exactly, but as exhaustion finally finding wisdom.

"For now."

Benvolio looked over the letter, the black drive, the dark monitor, and his own clean hands. It had started with Rosaline and a letter. Now, finally, the letter had reached everyone it needed to reach.

And if peace came, it would not be because the law had punished every wrong. It would be because, for once, it had refused to become one more weapon.

Epilogue. Sunday Morning — Beyond the District Line

Romeo woke to Juliet kissing him. For a soft, unreal instant, he thought the pain had invented her. Then her fingers touched the fresh bandage wrapped around his ribs, and her hair brushed his cheek.

"Don't move," she whispered.

"I wasn't."

"You were thinking about it."

"I think about many foolish things."

"Not today."

The bedroom was dim, lit only by a low amber lamp near the bed. Outside, rain tapped softly against the covered window. Somewhere beyond the door, Galina and Father Lawrence spoke in low voices, but for once the world stayed outside. Juliet kissed the bruise at his temple. Then the split at his mouth. Then the hollow beneath his jaw, where his pulse beat strong enough for her to feel.

Romeo closed his eyes. "You're checking if I'm real."

"Yes."

"And?"

She kissed him again, slower this time, deep enough that the ache in his side vanished beneath the ache of wanting her closer.

"You are," she said.

His hand found her waist. The movement pulled at the wound, and he drew a startled inhale.

Juliet lifted her head at once. "I told you not to move."

"You kissed me."

"That was medical."

"Was it?"

"I am very dedicated."

He almost laughed, but she pressed a hand gently over his mouth before the pain could catch him.

"Careful," she said.

Her voice broke on the word. Romeo saw her then and understood everything she was trying not to show: fear still bright in her eyes, grief held back by force, love so fierce it had become its own kind of trembling. He covered her hand with his.

"I'm here," he said.

Juliet nodded once, but tears slipped anyway.

He kissed her fingers. "So are you."

She lowered herself beside him carefully, fitting against his uninjured side. Romeo turned his face into her hair.

For a while, they only breathed. Juliet's hand rested over his heart. Romeo's fingers moved slowly through her hair. Outside, the dark thinned toward morning.

"What happens now?" he asked.

Juliet lifted her head. There was no innocence left in her face. No easy dream. Only love, bruised and alive, looking back at him with clear eyes.

"Now?" she whispered.

He waited. She kissed him once more, tender and certain.

"We live."

Made in the USA
Monee, IL
15 June 2026

54178059R00105